HAVEN

THE MAGIC EMPORIUM

A FOX HOLLOW NOVELLA

MORGAN BRICE

HAVEN
THE MAGIC EMPORIUM

A Fox Hollow Novella

By Morgan Brice

eBook ISBN: 978-1-64795-009-5
Paperback ISBN: 978-1-64795-066-8

Darkwind Press is an imprint of DreamSpinner Communications, LLC

1

AUSTIN

"I guess the directions were right, after all." Austin Williams parked his 4Runner in front of the chain-link fence and turned off the engine. He pulled an old photo out of the folder on the passenger seat and held it up for comparison against the view out his windshield.

Havenwood Psychiatric Hospital had seen better days. The photo dated from the 1950s and showed a well-maintained, sprawling Victorian-era facility, with gardens and a tree-shaded lawn.

The abandoned hulk behind the fence looked like the zombie version of its former self. Decades of neglect showed in peeling paint, broken windows, and vandals' tags. News articles Austin had printed out lamented that the old facility was too dated to renovate affordably and too solidly built to demolish.

Austin put the picture back in the folder and got out of the car. He walked to the fence and stared through the links at the decaying building on the hill, holding his breath as if he expected something to happen.

Fifteen-year-old Thomas McKean had vanished from

Havenwood in 1965. As it turned out, Thomas wasn't the only patient to go missing over the years. Austin had a list of twenty residents who had disappeared between 1960 and the hospital's closure. He suspected that the real number was far higher. The twenty people Austin identified so far had families who never stopped looking for answers, but some of the patients sent here had no one to notice their absence.

Austin's grandmother had begged her private detective grandson to solve the mystery of her brother's disappearance so she could die in peace.

"What the hell happened to you, Thomas?" Austin pocketed his keys and walked along the old fence, noting where it sagged or where thrill-seekers and urban explorers had clipped through links to make a hole big enough to wriggle through. He figured that sooner or later, his quest would require some minor breaking and entering for a good cause.

But not today. Austin wanted to get a feel for Saranac Lake, the northern Adirondack town that was home to Havenwood and several similar institutions. The other hospitals had specialized in treating tuberculosis, providing clean mountain air and restful surroundings for patients until modern medicine developed a cure. No one had vanished from the tuberculosis facilities.

That just confirmed Austin's suspicion that something had preyed upon Havenwood's vulnerable residents, people who had been institutionalized for mental illness—real and imagined.

They probably would have locked me up back then too, if they knew about my "hunches."

Austin's dreams sometimes showed him visions of moments in the past, present, and future. He'd come to trust his gut working on cases, but for him, that went far beyond the "intuition" cops and detectives credited with lucky hunches. He had also learned the hard way not to admit to having any extra abilities. That never went well.

Havenwood was a huge Kirkbride-style structure, with a three-story central building and large two-story wings on either side. It had been designed to provide a lot of natural light and air circulation and was surrounded by gardens and farmland—all part of the most progressive medical thinking of the late 1800s.

Too bad that in practice, places like this ended up being hellish instead of enlightened.

Austin's research hadn't turned up any convictions of staff associated with Havenwood, but that didn't mean neglect and abuse hadn't occurred. That was one reason he'd tried to talk Grandma Helen out of digging up the past. He feared that finding out Thomas's fate might be worse than not knowing.

As he circled the building, Austin noted where the boards over some of the windows and doors looked loose and where unboarded windows had been broken. Once he had checked into what he could learn at the local library and historical association, Austin had no doubts that he would be back for a first-hand peek inside. Even if he didn't find answers for his grandma, she might take comfort in photos of places Thomas would have found familiar.

Austin tried to imagine what the building and its grounds had looked like in its heyday. The black and white photos and grainy resolution didn't do the place justice. Whatever had befallen Thomas, Austin hoped that his great-uncle had been able to take some solace in the natural beauty.

By the time he returned to his car, Austin's mood had turned pensive, remembering Grandma Helen's account of the night Thomas was taken away. She was eight years younger than her brother, so her memories were patchy and filtered through a child's understanding.

She'd told him that there had been some sort of altercation, and then men in strange uniforms took Thomas away in the night, restrained in what she now realized had been a straitjacket. Her parents never spoke of him again and refused to answer her questions, even when she was an adult. She'd found what little paperwork she'd given Austin after her parents died, locked away in the safe like a shameful secret.

He left the abandoned hospital and drove into the town of Saranac Lake, taking in the quaint architecture and eyeing the shops and restaurants, although he didn't expect his visit to allow much time for sightseeing. Still, he'd need to eat, and several of the cafés looked good, plus Austin spotted a coffee shop he intended to visit tomorrow morning. With its picturesque buildings nestled between the lake and mountains, the village looked ready-made for postcards.

Austin checked in at the Lake Shore Inn, a vintage mom-and-pop one-story motel that had a 1930s vibe. He'd have preferred a room at the historic Hotel Saranac, but that wasn't in the budget, especially since Grandma Helen wasn't a paying client.

"Welcome to the Lake Shore. I'm Greg, the owner. How can I help you?" The man at the front desk greeted Austin with a cheery smile.

"Austin Williams. I've got a reservation."

The front office's classic pine paneling and camp-style decor looked homey and authentic—just like the man behind the counter, a fellow in his sixties with short gray hair and a full silver beard. His bright blue eyes looked younger than the weather-lined face.

"Did you have a particular room theme in mind?" Greg asked.

Austin looked at him blankly. "Theme?"

Greg grinned. "The decor is rather whimsical, but people like it, and so we've kept it the same over the years. Each room has a different theme—some of them are local wildlife, birds, or fish, or there are important historic tidbits."

"Um, I'll take the wildlife," Austin replied. "Surprise me."

"What brings you to town, Mr. Williams?" Greg asked as he ran Austin's credit card and handed him the sign-in paperwork.

"My grandparents used to vacation here," Austin lied pleasantly. "They talked about the town so much; I had to come see for myself."

"I'm not surprised," Greg replied, handing back his card. "This town gets into your blood. Lots of families come back year after year. How long are you staying?"

"I don't know," Austin answered with a smile. "Figured I'd see the sights, enjoy the scenery, and play it by ear. Had a bunch of vacation time that was use-it or lose-it, so for the next couple of weeks, I'm a man of leisure."

Since Austin worked for himself, he didn't have to clear vacation time with anyone, but the answer satisfied Greg and provided wiggle room to change his plans. No one needed to know that Austin was tracing what was likely to be either murder or gross negligence. Small towns had long memories.

Which meant Greg could be a useful resource if they hit

it off. Austin could be a tough SOB when necessary, but he also knew how to be charming.

"What's your favorite place to eat?" Austin returned Greg's smile. "I had a long drive, and I'm starving."

"Depends on what you want," Greg answered and shrugged. "The dining room at Hotel Saranac is top of the line if you want a great steak, cloth napkins, and all the extras."

"Maybe something a little more affordable," Austin replied and chuckled. "I'm more of a budget traveler."

"We've got you covered. Sciallo's Restaurant is locally owned, homemade Greek-Italian food, big portions, reasonable prices. You can always bring leftovers back with you and heat them in the microwave in your room," Greg added. "Benny's Grill is on the lakeshore and serves plenty of fresh fish and bar food done well. It's a local favorite, and there's a drink special every night. White Wolf Coffee and Beer roasts its own beans and does pastries for breakfast, then in the evening it's a pretty darn good brew pub, with an awesome venison burger."

Greg slid a map of the downtown across the counter. "There are more places, but those are my favorites. Plenty of stuff is in walking distance from here, which is nice when the weather's good like today."

"I was just going to head downtown and do a little exploring," Austin replied. He looked at the map. "Are the library and historical association on here?"

Greg grabbed a pen and circled two locations. "Yep. Better check the hours though, because they vary. I hope you have a great day." His enthusiasm cajoled Austin out of his earlier pensive mood.

"You too," Austin replied. "Thanks a lot." He took the map and grabbed his key card, then drove over to park in front of his unit. When he opened the door, Austin felt pleasantly surprised that the room was even nicer than the photos online.

The galley kitchen wasn't fancy, but it had a fridge, microwave, coffee maker, and two-burner stove, so he didn't have to eat out for every meal, and the table with four chairs made a decent workspace. A comfortable couch faced a working fireplace Austin couldn't wait to use. The small patio looked out over the lake. Best of all was the king-size bed that meant Austin wouldn't have to curl his six-foot-one frame into a ball so his feet didn't hang off.

The only thing he wasn't sure about was the taxidermied moose head on the wall. He'd obviously gotten the "moose" room. Photos of moose, a hand-painted moose mural, moose-printed drapes, and a buffalo plaid comforter on the king bed with a moose outline made the theme impossible to overlook. Even the mugs in the kitchen had a moose face on them.

"I guess it could be worse," he muttered. "Could have been the skunk room or the trout room. But that moose head is creepy." Austin went into the bathroom, grabbed one of the extra towels, and tossed it over the moose's face, so he didn't feel quite so watched by those glassy eyes.

He dropped his duffel bag on the end of the bed and returned to the bathroom to freshen up after his drive from Albany. The generously-sized shower got a nod of approval, and he hoped it had good pressure and plenty of hot water. Austin relieved his full bladder, then bent over the sink to splash water on his face.

The brown eyes that stared back at him in the mirror looked tired and worn. Austin hadn't realized how much his lack of sleep showed until he stopped to look at his reflection and saw the dark shadows beneath his eyes. *Visions don't make for a good night's sleep.*

Austin ran a hand through his short, dark blond hair to ruffle it back into place. At thirty-five, he'd gained some crinkles next to his eyes when he smiled. The black T-shirt under his long-sleeved flannel accentuated a muscular chest, and his worn jeans hugged a toned ass and strong thighs. He wasn't a bodybuilder, but the workouts he'd learned as an Albany cop kept him in fighting shape; useful, since private investigators didn't tend to hang out with model citizens.

The nightmares had started once he agreed to Grandma Helen's quest.

He saw images of people and places he didn't recognize, but he knew in his gut they had something to do with Thomas's case. That was how his questionable psychic abilities worked and one of the reasons his close rate on cold cases was exceptional. The visions—waking or sleeping—were brief, fragmented, like a puzzle to be pieced together. Faces, locations, sometimes a clock or calendar—Austin knew from experience that if he was patient and did the legwork to connect the dots, the answer would come. *Not always a happy answer, but that's out of my control.*

His hunches had cost Austin his job as a detective, despite—or because of—a stellar success rate. Jealousy and suspicion led to ugly rumors about how Austin managed to solve cases that had stumped plenty of good cops for years. There'd been whispers—all untrue—to "explain" how he succeeded when others failed. The stories that circulated were crazy—payoffs, blackmail, torture, even trading favors with criminal kingpins. Outlandish rumors that overlooked hard work, dogged persistence, and a bit of a "shine," as Grandma Helen called his talent.

He knew he couldn't admit to the visions, and eventually he tired of the jealousy, so he quit the force and got his investigator's license. The Albany cops didn't make it easy for him, but they'd eventually worked out a fragile truce.

Austin dried his face and stepped out onto the porch, looking out over the lake toward the mountains beyond. *God, it's gorgeous here. I wish I could stay.*

He took a deep breath of the balsam-scented air and listened to the screech of a loon in the distance, somewhere out on the lake. If his gut was right—and it always was—the town's natural beauty hid dark secrets. Sticking around after he got answers probably wouldn't be healthy.

The images from his dreams and visions swirled in his mind. *What do I know? I saw a long institutional corridor— probably Havenwood. An older man—maybe a doctor? A middle-aged woman with her hair pinned up, probably a nurse. A panel truck, driving off into the night.*

Those images had a faded tinge, meaning they were from the past. One other image—in vivid color, present-day —also haunted him. More than once he'd seen a brown-haired man close to his own age in a darkened building, clearly frightened. It wasn't much to go on, although Austin thought he'd recognize the man if he ever saw him for real. As for who he was, how he might be connected to the case, or why he was afraid—that was a mystery.

But damn if just that glimpse hadn't caught his interest in a highly unprofessional way. The stranger had riveting light blue eyes, hair long enough to get a good grip, and plush pink lips made for kissing. The way the man's gaze locked with Austin's in the vision, begging for help, triggered something overprotective and a little possessively Neanderthal, a crazy desire to rescue and claim that always woke him breathless and hard.

Just thinking about the mysterious stranger left Austin with a semi that forced him to adjust his jeans. "Been too damn long since I got laid," he muttered as if that explained away the image.

Austin's stomach growled, and he turned away from the view. It was time to get a feel for this town and see what the local records might have to say about Havenwood.

But first, food.

Austin strolled into downtown Saranac Lake, pausing now and then to window shop. The eclectic variety of stores and bistros could only work in a tourist town. He appreciated the mix of Victorian-era architecture with creatively modernized buildings and loved the glimpses he got of the lake in the distance.

The luscious smells made his stomach growl when he opened the door to Benny's Grill. The lunch crowd had come and gone, except for a few latecomers scattered throughout the dining room. Austin requested a table in the back and took his time going through the menu. Everything looked good. If he ended up staying in town chasing leads, at least he wouldn't starve.

He ordered the venison burger with potato planks and a cup of coffee to bump him out of an afternoon slump. Habit had him scanning the small crowd of patrons, trying to get a feel for the locals. Research could only explain so much; the best recon happened with boots on the ground.

Most of the people he had seen so far favored upscale brands of outdoor clothing, the kind bought at specialty stores that also sold skis and high-end equipment. That was a contrast to the more rugged towns that sported a no-nonsense flannel-and-jeans vibe. At least the clothing he'd packed—his nicer outdoor casual options—fit right in.

People tended to answer questions more easily from someone who looked the part.

Like Lake Placid and Lake George, Saranac Lake had been a favored vacation spot for the robber barons of the Gilded Age. Unlike the other towns, part of Saranac's fame came from its "healthful air" and innovative treatments for tuberculosis, which struck rich and poor alike. The well-off could afford to "take the cure" by going to the mountains, to private hospitals with the amenities of a fine hotel.

That made Havenwood an anomaly, he mused since it had catered to those with broken minds instead of ravaged lungs. Havenwood had been a public hospital, which made it a place of last resort for those who had no family to look after them or whose families had turned their backs.

Austin toyed with the paper straw wrapper as his thoughts spun. Grandma Helen didn't know why Thomas was sent away. She hadn't seen her brother get out of hand, and she had no memory of him being drunk. In her memory, everything seemed normal and fine—until suddenly, it wasn't.

There's a missing piece, something that we aren't seeing. That's what I need to find to make sense of things.

As he sipped his soda, Austin glanced around the room once more. His gaze halted on a man at a table near the windows, and he almost choked.

That's him! That's the guy from my vision. Except he doesn't look like he's in danger.

Austin took a deep breath and forced himself to focus. Now that he got a better look, he figured the man was in his late twenties or early thirties, making him five or six years younger than Austin. His chestnut hair had highlights and was just the right length for someone to tangle their fingers in during intimate moments.

I wonder if his hair is as silky as it looks. I bet it would be soft. I bet he'd get off having it tugged while he was giving head...

Austin closed his eyes, trying to stop his mind from continuing down a frustrating, pointless path. *I might be able to protect him, warn him, save him. That doesn't mean I'm going to sleep with him.*

But I'd really like to.

That surprised Austin because it had been a while since anyone had caught his interest. His last relationship had ended a year ago. The parting had been amicable, both of them realizing that they weren't a good match for the long haul. Breaking up had been the right choice, but it still left Austin lonely, wondering if he would ever find his "forever" person.

Most of the time, Austin could push those thoughts out of his mind, staying busy with work. He hadn't bothered to look for a hook-up to take the edge off in longer than he could remember. That made his reaction to the handsome stranger even more surprising since no one else had caught his attention in quite a while.

"Here's your burger," his server said, bringing his meal. It looked as good as it smelled, and Austin's mouth watered at the aroma. "Can I refill your drink and get you some ketchup for those potatoes?"

Austin answered her questions distractedly, wishing that she didn't block his view of the man by the window. He was trying to concoct a reason to introduce himself or to strike up a conversation without looking like a stalker.

"Just let me know if you need something," she said, finally moving out of the way.

Austin's heart sank as he realized that the man from his vision was gone.

The burger was exceptional, but Austin had lost his

appetite. He ate quickly, wolfing down his food like a starving man, and promised himself that on his next visit he'd take his time. Over and over, his gaze strayed to the empty table.

Should I ask the server? Maybe she knows him. But what reason could I give that doesn't sound creepy?

He didn't want it to get around that a private investigator was in town. That would derail his efforts and compromise his reason for coming here before he even got started. And Austin certainly didn't want to leave the impression that the man from his vision might have done something wrong or was under investigation.

All of which left him frustrated and annoyed. *Still, maybe he's a regular. If I'm here tomorrow at the same time, I could come up with a reason to talk to him. This is a small town. The odds are good we'll cross paths again. He showed up in my vision for a reason.*

Austin settled his bill and headed for the local library. The small building was a focus of the community, if the bulletin board at the front was any indication. Flyers promoted a wealth of local events, fundraisers, and small businesses. Business cards were pinned for the taking. Austin figured that the folks who lived here year-round were a close-knit bunch, good at supporting each other while also being self-sufficient.

That didn't bode well for prying secrets loose.

Austin had called ahead to make an appointment with the head librarian, under the guise of doing genealogical research. He'd eventually work the conversation around to obituaries, cemetery records, and Havenwood. Austin held no illusions about how well poking around in the past was likely to be received.

He found his way to the librarian's office. Austin had

done some homework ahead of time, wanting to know who he would be dealing with. Harold Winters was in his sixties and had worked for the library for thirty years. He was a Saranac Lake native, related to half the town—and his father had worked in the records department at Havenwood during the time when Thomas was a patient.

That meant the odds were good that Winters knew something about the long-ago disappearances, either from hearsay or first-hand. He was also likely to know the people responsible. At some point, Austin would need to find out whether Winters would welcome the chance to unburden himself.

"Mr. Williams. How can I be of help?" Winters said all the right things, but his body language told Austin that the librarian resented the interruption. Winters waved Austin toward a chair in front of the desk.

"As I mentioned in my email, I'm doing some genealogy research," Austin said. "You know how it is—no one gets interested in family history until the people who had a lot of the answers have passed on."

Winters nodded. "That's more common than you might think. Such a shame."

Years of interviewing suspects had honed Austin's skill at interpreting non-verbal cues. Winters was impatient and edgy while trying not to appear as either. *Maybe he's just an asshole, or maybe he doesn't like out-of-towners poking around.*

"Even with all the tools on the internet, it's hard to fill in the blanks," Austin said. "But I found a name, Thomas McKean, with a note about Saranac Lake. This would have been back in the 1960s." He spread his hands, palms up, in a gesture of frustration. "So here I am, chasing a ghost."

"That's not much to go on."

Austin shook his head. "No, it isn't." He'd already

decided to play dumb, look as harmless as possible, and try to figure out the players before tipping his hand. "I did all I could online and figured that there might be resources here that hadn't been digitized. I'll be thrilled with anything I can find."

"We have a newspaper archive going back even farther than the 1960s," Winters replied. "Nothing before 1995 is online. Some of the old issues were put on microfiche, but the money ran out, and the rest is still in paper format, bound into yearly volumes."

"I'm willing to dig. It's a bit of an adventure," Austin replied. "What about tax records or deeds?" He knew that Thomas wouldn't show up in those documents, but he wanted to look like he was covering all the bases.

"Anything that was available to the public should be with our government documents," the librarian told him. "I'll warn you—there's not a lot of call for that kind of thing, and I can't promise we've dusted down there recently."

"A few sneezes are worth it," Austin assured him. "How about cemetery records? I couldn't find anything online for those either." He didn't intend to mention that he had sent a request to the county for a death certificate and found nothing.

"Probably at the main offices for the particular cemeteries," Winters replied. "Not something we'd have here except for those buried on state property, but that's mostly prisoners and John Does, which isn't going to be what you're looking for."

Since Havenwood was a state-run hospital, that's exactly what I need, Austin thought, but he kept his expression neutral. "I'll tackle visiting the cemeteries another day then. He might not have even been in Saranac Lake when he died. That's part of what I'm trying to find out."

"The newspaper morgue is in the basement, and that's where you'll find the microfiche readers," Winters said. "The old public records aren't locked away—they're just not something we get much interest in. I wish you luck." His tone made it clear he couldn't care less.

Austin thanked him and left the office, heading downstairs. He'd taken a risk calling attention to himself with Winters, but he wanted to get a read on the man before the time came to ask hard questions.

The records room's fluorescent lights made the gray, featureless area feel cold and sterile. Austin worked his way along the shelves, finding the newspapers and other documents from the right time period. He brought the heavy bound tomes to the worktable and pulled up a stool.

"Let's start with obituaries," he muttered. TV detectives made the work look glamorous and easy, but the reality was much more likely to require hours or days searching through old records than getting involved in high-speed car chases.

All Austin had to go on was the date on the letter his great grandfather had received from Havenwood letting them know that Thomas had "run away" and was no longer a patient at the facility. He didn't expect to find Thomas mentioned by name in any of the records, but any note about an unnamed juvenile—in the police blotter or as an unclaimed body—might give him something to work with.

He had a list of the other patients who had disappeared, with a best guess of when they had gone missing. If he had to comb through dusty old records, he hoped to only have to do it once. That meant working through all the names and dates in each type of record before moving on to the next set and starting all over again.

"What the hell?" he muttered as he flipped through the

old newspapers within several days of Thomas's disappearance, checking the police blotter. All of the papers were complete except for one—which was missing only that page.

Austin quickly checked the archived papers for the other missing patients, only to discover that in each case, the newspaper had a page removed for the police news on a date within a few days of the disappearance.

"Fuck." He replaced the oversized, bound newspapers and pulled out the death records. Havenwood's deaths showed up in the listing, but here and there, a month would be missing, or the page from a particular month that would have included the hospital's information.

One or two missing pages could have been accidental damage. But every single one? Too much of a coincidence.

A chilling thought occurred to him. *I doubt I have a complete list of everyone who disappeared. If I found other missing pages, does that indicate more people?*

How did so many patients vanish? Did they die under questionable circumstances, and Havenwood just told families they disappeared? Was security so bad that patients could simply walk away? And what kind of conditions had they been committed for in the first place?

Austin knew that in the not-so-olden days, lack of information and prejudice about mental health meant that people were all too often sent away for being "inconvenient" or because their illness embarrassed family members. Many of those conditions were easily treatable now, but the causes eluded medical professionals back then. *And some of them didn't really try too hard to understand.*

The list of names Austin had compiled were of people whose families had remained in contact—however tenuous —with Havenwood. But a public hospital would have also taken in orphans or adults without family to care for them who were judged to be odd or difficult.

How many of them went missing and no one was ever notified? They just disappeared—and were forgotten.

He sighed. *Focus on Thomas. I can't change what happened more than half a century ago, and the hospital closed, so it's not hurting anyone new. If I find out about Thomas, it might give me a good idea about the others. I can give the families closure, at least. For what it's worth.*

Austin glanced at his watch after he cleaned up the worktable. The afternoon had flown by, and it was already four o'clock.

I won't get much done at the Historical Association, but maybe I can at least find out who's in charge. The website was vague about that.

He trudged upstairs and nearly collided with Harold Winters.

"Did you find what you were looking for?" Winters's bland voice meant that he either really didn't care or that he was utterly dead inside. Austin hadn't figured out which was more likely.

"Mostly, yes," Austin replied. "Although I was surprised to find so many missing pages in the records. That seemed...odd."

Winters's eyes narrowed. "What do you mean?"

Austin shrugged, not ready to make any accusations just yet. "I couldn't figure out why pages were missing in some sections and not others. I hope no one vandalized the records."

"Old documents are fragile. Accidents happen, despite our best attempts at preservation." Winters's voice lost all pretense of friendliness.

"I'm sure that's it," Austin murmured. "That's the thing

about poking around in the past—you never know what you're going to find, do you?"

"Sometimes, for the best."

Austin wondered if it was just his imagination, detecting a threat in Winters's statement. He gave Winters his most engaging smile, just to confuse the shit out of him. "Probably so," he agreed. "Anyhow—thank you for your help. Depending on what else I find, I might be back."

He could have sworn he felt the weight of Winters's gaze on him as he headed out the door. *I notice he didn't say "come back anytime." Did he guess that Thomas had a connection to Havenwood? Or maybe he just doesn't like outsiders.*

By the time Austin walked to the Historical Association, it was nearly four-thirty. The large brick Victorian converted house retained its charm and had obviously been well-maintained. A sign on the door with the daily hours confirmed that closing time was at five.

That's all right. Maybe I can at least size the place up.

The old house smelled like books and lavender. A small display of glass cases near the front featured items from notable events in the town's history, while posters on a bulletin board in the foyer highlighted local lectures, book signings, art displays, and musical performances.

Austin couldn't help feeling pleased that the organization hadn't tried to hollow out the old house to change its purpose. Instead, one room flowed into the next, complete with period artwork and seating areas featuring modern versions of Victorian-style furnishings. The association must have generous donors, Austin thought, noting that nothing looked shabby or hard-worn. That was a pleasant change from many other archives he had visited.

"Hello?" he called out when he reached the archivist's vacant desk. Austin wasn't surprised not to see other patrons a half hour before closing. But he had hoped to meet the person whose favor he would need to curry to get access to the Historical Association's documents.

"Be with you in a minute!" a voice called from the next room. A moment later, a dark-haired man emerged, carrying a stack of old books. "How can I help you?" he asked with a friendly smile.

Austin found himself at a loss for words, staring at the man from the restaurant—the one whose face haunted his dreams and who his visions warned was in danger.

"I'm not completely sure..." he managed.

2

JAMIE

The handsome stranger looked a bit pole-axed, staring at Jamie in surprised recognition although he didn't seem familiar.

"We'll be closing at five, but we open tomorrow at nine," he offered, wondering if the man was lost.

The newcomer smiled, and Jamie's heart sped up. Short, dark blond hair, pretty brown eyes, and broad shoulders got his attention right away. So did the toned chest that tapered to narrow hips beneath the man's sweater and jacket. He definitely caught Jamie's notice, something that hadn't happened often since he'd moved to Saranac Lake.

"I realize it's close to quitting time, but I wondered if I could meet the archivist? Then we can pick up in the morning."

Jamie chuckled. "That would be me. Temporary archivist Jamie Miller, at your service."

Hmm...I wouldn't mind "servicing" him. Guys like that don't wander in places like this every day.

The newcomer smiled and stepped close enough to shake hands. "Austin Williams. I'm doing some genealogical research, and I'm hoping you can help me. It's a bit like solving a mystery—I've got bits and pieces, but I need to find the glue to hold them together."

Austin's hand was warm and the palm more calloused than Jamie had expected. His first guess had been that the man was a professor or researcher, but the callouses suggested a more hands-on vocation. *Maybe I can get some answers while I'm helping him with his "bits and pieces."*

Jamie almost felt guilty about lusting after the man, but he'd had a long dry spell, and Austin was the best thing to come along in quite a while.

"We're still open for twenty minutes. Tell me what you're looking for, and that way I can think about it overnight so we can get a jumpstart tomorrow." Jamie waived Austin toward a seat at a study table.

Jamie listened as Austin talked about his great-uncle's disappearance and his grandmother's desire for answers. He asked a few questions, most of which Austin said he didn't know the answers to. When Austin fell silent, Jamie leaned back in his chair, sad to find that they only had a few minutes left before he needed to close up.

"I'm happy to help you, but the kind of records that might help you find your great-uncle would be at the county courthouse or the library," Jamie said. "Especially if he wasn't from a local family, I don't think anything we'd have here will be what you need."

Austin hesitated like he was trying to decide whether he should confide in Jamie. "I think he might have been a patient at Havenwood," he said quietly. "I thought the archive might be able to shed some light on the hospital in that period."

"Oh." Jamie had only been at the archive for a month, but he'd already heard plenty of whispers about Havenwood, the creepy old abandoned hospital on the edge of town. "That's a bit of a touchy subject. What are you hoping to find?"

Havenwood had been closed for decades, but plenty of people in town had worked there, and many of those former employees were still alive. Jamie had overheard some heated arguments between long-time residents over the rumors that still circulated about the old mental institution. He had steered clear since he was just filling in until a permanent archivist could be found. But he figured that both sides probably had a bit of truth to them. A place that big with such a long history dealing with vulnerable people was bound to have some heroes and villains.

Which made him wonder what Austin was *really* hoping to find.

The alarm on Jamie's phone went off, telling him it was time to lock up. "I have to close on time," Jamie said, sorry to bring the conversation to an end. "Our insurance company won't let me stay open beyond the posted times or have anyone inside after we're closed."

Austin rose. "I understand. Thanks for listening. I'll be glad for any help." He paused. "One more question— where's a good place to get a bite to eat?" he asked with a slightly shy smile that sent a surge of heat to Jamie's groin.

"Do you like pizza? Moosehead Inn is a locals' joint that serves great food. I was going to head over once I lock up— you're welcome to join me if you don't have other plans," Jamie offered, trying to sound nonchalant.

Did I just ask him out? Holy shit. I haven't done that in...forever.

Austin brightened, and his smile grew broader. "I'd like that. I'll wait outside. Can we walk there? I didn't bring my car."

Jamie nodded, still a little surprised at his own boldness. "Sure. See you in a few minutes."

He ushered Austin out the door and locked it behind him. Fortunately, Jamie had gotten a head start on the lock-up checklist before the sexy stranger arrived. He powered down the computer and started flipping off light switches as he made his way toward the back door.

This was the part he really disliked. Once he turned on the alarm system, the security lights would come on. But on the way to the back door, the old house got darker, and the shadows stretched longer with every switch he flicked.

I thought I knew what I was getting into when I took the job. But it's just temporary, and I'm still sending out applications for something better, he reminded himself.

An old house like this was likely to have ghosts, even without being turned into a museum of sorts. Bring together the personal belongings of hundreds of people, bits of local history, journals, and letters, and it didn't surprise Jamie that the place was haunted. Even if no one else seemed to believe it.

Click, click, click. He turned off the lights in the foyer and the former sitting room and dining room. Jamie had closed up the upstairs rooms early since it was a slow day. It held a storage area, a library of books written by local authors and books about the Saranac Lake area, as well as a conference room and a small classroom for lectures. The attic and base-ment were storage areas that weren't open to the public, which made Jamie very happy since both gave him the creeps.

Click. The lights in the old parlor went dark, and Jamie braced himself. On the nights the ghosts felt frisky, this was when the *shenanigans* started.

A cool breeze out of nowhere made the hair on the back

of Jamie's neck rise. He heard the glissando of crystal pendants gently bumping together, the decorative dangles on a vintage oil lamp in the parlor that shouldn't have any reason to move.

Jamie resolutely ignored the shadow gliding just at the edge of his peripheral vision as he hurried down the hallway. The kitchen doubled as the staff room and was the least haunted place in the building. Jamie heard footsteps on the stairs and forced himself to breathe. He knew there was no one else in the old house—at least, no one living.

In the room to his left by the back door, the former sewing room for the ladies of the house, he glimpsed a familiar gray figure and heard the swish of crinoline and linen. To his right, in the small office that was once the cook's room, a rocking chair creaked.

Jamie's hand shook as he set the alarm. The ghosts didn't act up every night, and some evenings they were more riled than others. So far, none of them had tried to hurt him. As unsettling as the ghostly manifestations were, Jamie couldn't object to spirits wanting to stay in a place that meant something to them. He didn't mess with them, and he hoped that meant they would return the favor.

The alarm beeped, and the security lights came on, dim but enough to send the shadows scurrying. The sounds stopped, and the house grew quiet. Jamie slipped out the back door and checked the lock, then let out a long breath. The halogen light above the door made the area around the steps almost as bright as day. He shook off the weirdness and smiled, excited about dinner with Austin.

It's not a date. But I wish it was. Maybe... This could be a pleasant diversion, Jamie told himself. Austin was just in town to look up some family history, and Jamie's role with the archive was temporary. Nothing said they couldn't have a little fun while their paths crossed.

"Everything okay?" Austin asked when Jamie came around to the front.

Jamie nodded, eager to put the ghostly activity out of mind. That was definitely not a conversation for a first date. Or maybe, ever. "Yeah. You know how it is. There's a whole list of things to check and turn off before I can leave. No big deal."

The night had grown colder, and Jamie was glad for his warm parka and soft scarf. Austin was equally hidden beneath plenty of layers. "I'm from Albany. Gets cold there, but I think you get more snow up here," Austin said.

Jamie chuckled. "I grew up in Rochester, which is no slouch when it comes to snow. But up here, there's still more. Although I don't know that I'll be in town for the whole winter. We'll have to see," he said, and his breath clouded in the cold air.

"Didn't you say you'd just started at the archive?" Austin gave him a puzzled glance.

"My position is temporary," Jamie explained. "I've got all the right credentials except one—I'm not from around here. They want someone from the general area, but they needed to keep the Historical Association running while they do their search, so they brought me in to fill the gap."

"That's too bad. I mean, if you like it here," Austin replied, and Jamie thought the other man sounded a little nervous.

Maybe I'm not the only one who hasn't been on a date for a while. If this is a date. Maybe it will turn into one if I'm lucky.

"It's nice, at least for a change," Jamie said. "I needed to get out of Rochester and try something new. I grew up there, went to college and grad school there—too much of a good thing, you know?"

"Yeah, I get it," Austin agreed.

They bumped shoulders as they walked, and Jamie liked how natural being with Austin felt. He didn't feel pressure to make himself seem more exciting or a need to justify his professional choices.

"I did my Ph.D. in History—specializing in the Victorian Era. I'd like to teach eventually, but right out of school, I was working on projects with the historic home museums in the city to 'humanize' them—find and acquire family heirlooms that belonged in the houses, use journals, photos, and letters to make a house's appearance as close as possible to how it was when the family lived there. That sort of thing." He left out the part about how seeing ghosts came with the territory.

Jamie realized he was rambling and shut his mouth. But instead of making a wisecrack like Jamie's last boyfriend, Austin looked at him with genuine interest. "That's pretty cool. I can see the connection. I've always liked history."

Was Austin flirting? Jamie hoped so.

"How about you?" he asked as they reached Moosehead Inn. The place had been around since the 1940s, gradually building on extra rooms in a crazy-quilt floor plan. Pine paneled walls, a vintage mahogany bar, and an elaborate barback that rumor held came out of a brothel in Schenectady gave it plenty of character. A taxidermied moose head complete with antlers hung in a place of honor in the dining area.

Austin waited to answer until they were at their table in a corner. Austin claimed the seat with his back to the wall. He glanced all around, and Jamie figured he was taking in the atmosphere. Then he realized that Austin's narrowed gaze looked like he was scanning for danger. That made him wonder where the other man had needed to learn that level of caution.

"I was a cop and worked up to detective," Austin said as if he guessed Jamie's unspoken questions. "Got tired of the politics and became a private investigator. Same skills, but better hours, and my new boss isn't quite as much of an asshole," he added with a self-deprecating smile.

"Is it as glamorous as in the movies?" Jamie teased.

"Is being a historian like in *The DaVinci Code*?"

"Heavens, no!" Jamie replied. "Those guys break into museums and get shot at. Most of us dig through old journals and local records to put together the pieces of history's jigsaw puzzle."

"That's a great way to put it," Austin said, and his brown eyes were warm with interest. "I guess we have that in common. Being a detective—or an investigator—is a lot of research. More Google than gunfights, which is a good thing, I guess."

A server came for their drink order, which reminded them to look at the menu. "Everything I've had here has been awesome," Jamie said. "There's a bison burger if plain old beef doesn't do it for you, and a Reuben that's pretty legit. The fried pickles are a specialty, and the soft pretzels are house made. I'm partial to the potato soup," he added with a grin, feeling his stomach rumble.

Austin got the Reuben, Jamie went for the burger, and they split a soft pretzel and an order of fried pickles between them. They both ordered beer, and Jamie was pleased that Austin took his recommendation for one of the local microbrews the bar carried.

"This stuff is really good," Austin said after he'd had a sip, sounding mildly surprised.

"The Moose is pretty picky when it comes to beer," Jamie replied with a laugh. "That's what the locals call the place. Took me a while to realize they didn't mean a real moose—because we have a lot of those around here too. They're a menace on the road."

The last time Jamie had been on a date, it had been someone he'd swiped right on in an app. The evening had felt artificial, his companion couldn't stop checking his phone, and conversation sputtered to a halt. *At least that avoided any awkward discussion about sex.*

But even though he'd met Austin by chance barely an hour ago, this felt entirely different. Somehow the conversation just flowed, and even though they came from different backgrounds, they managed to find common ground. Like talking about favorite movies and ways to spend free time.

"The thing I like about superhero movies," Austin said around a mouthful of his sandwich, in answer to Jamie's question about his interests, "is that the good guys always win in the end. It doesn't happen much in real life."

"That's what I like about reading mysteries and romance," Jamie admitted. "The bad guy gets caught, and the lucky lovers get a happily ever after. I also really like shows about spooky stuff and ghost hunters. Maybe it's because so many historic homes are supposed to be haunted." *And in my experience, most of them are.*

He'd jumped in feet first and admitted his geeky side, almost daring Austin to take issue. He bet Austin had played sports in high school, maybe college. Some of the stereotypes about geeks and jocks were true, in Jamie's experience. Better to find out up front and cut his losses if it turned out that way.

"I love those shows too," Austin agreed, to Jamie's surprise. His enthusiasm seemed genuine. "I like the idea of riding around, exploring abandoned old buildings, shooting ghosts, and hunting werewolves. That's way more exciting than tracking down cheating husbands and insurance fraud."

Jamie watched Austin over the rim of his pint of beer. "You don't like your job?"

Austin shrugged and tore off a piece of pretzel, jabbing it into the nacho cheese. "Sometimes. I try to only take the cases that sound interesting, but some months you take what comes in the door if you want to eat. I like figuring out what's really going on, finding the missing pieces. On the downside, you don't always meet upstanding citizens," he added with a snort.

"But sometimes, you can help people, like your grandma," Jamie prompted.

Austin nodded. "On good days, yeah. I tried to talk her out of this, you know. When a person's been missing as long as Thomas has...well, the odds aren't in favor of one of those happy endings. Finding out might be worse than not knowing."

Jamie frowned, thinking. "Maybe. But I can understand wanting to know for sure. Fifty-some years is a long time to wonder."

"I guess." Austin didn't sound convinced. They had finished their food, but neither man seemed in a hurry to leave.

"You play pool—or darts?" Jamie asked, with a nod toward the back room, where several tables and targets awaited players.

"Both—badly. I'm marginally better at pool, but I'd hate to have to hustle money to eat. I'd be a lot thinner," Austin replied.

That made Jamie laugh, and he realized it had been a

while since he'd done that. "My dorm had a rec room in the basement with darts, pool, and Foosball," he said. "Playing was my way to unwind after classes. I logged a lot of hours down there." *And burned off plenty of frustration since my campus didn't have much of a gay social life.*

"C'mon," Jamie urged after they paid their checks. "Let's play a couple of rounds. Unless you're in a hurry to get back..."

Austin shook his head. "Not really. Nothing waiting at the room except the motel TV channels. This sounds like more fun." He caught Jamie's eye, and that twinkle was definitely interest.

"You're on!"

Two games of pool and four rounds of darts later, Jamie realized that Austin might have understated his skills with a cue stick since he'd handily won at the table. On the other hand, Jamie won three out of four of the dart games without trying too hard. He liked that it never got truly competitive, with neither one of them caring about winning or losing.

Austin was easy to be with, and Jamie felt more comfortable after an evening together than he had during some of his entire past relationships. With his exes, there had always been some part of himself he needed to keep hidden to fit in. He didn't feel like that with Austin, other than deciding not to talk about seeing ghosts.

If this turns into a little fling while he's in town, he doesn't need to know about the ghosts. Not like I'm keeping something from a steady partner. Why let something that doesn't matter get in the way of having fun while it lasts?

Part of Jamie felt sad that any relationship between the two of them came with a built-in expiration date. Then again, something this good didn't come along every day.

Jamie knew that for a fact, and he was determined to enjoy it.

"Since we've both got work to do in the morning, I guess we'd better call it a night," Austin said, rousing Jamie from his thoughts. They had finished their beers a while ago, but that didn't seem to affect Austin's tendency to stand a little too close, something Jamie hoped wasn't purely accidental. Jamie thought he heard regret in Austin's voice that the evening was coming to a close.

"I don't know about you, but I feel the need to eat something every night," Jamie joked. "Company is always welcome."

Austin returned his smile. "I might take you up on that."

The temperature had dropped even further by the time they left Moosehead Inn, making Jamie glad for his gloves and hood. Austin was bundled up as well, rocking what Jamie thought of as the "hot arctic explorer" look.

If polar bears can find a mate that's sexy under all that fur and fluff, I can use my imagination to picture what's underneath a down parka.

Austin insisted on walking Jamie back to his apartment, half of a renovated duplex. When Jamie had been offered the temporary position, a furnished apartment in addition to the salary had sweetened the deal. He had initially feared the offer meant an apartment on the top floor of the archive, and he'd been relieved to discover that wasn't the case. Jamie could deal with ghosts, but he didn't necessarily want to live with them.

When they reached the porch, Jamie felt strangely awkward. A kiss didn't seem like the right move since he wasn't sure they'd really been on a date, but even so, he felt a pang of disappointment.

"Guess I'll see you tomorrow morning," Austin said,

rocking a bit onto the balls of his feet as if he also felt the attraction.

"Bring coffee," Jamie teased. "I'm not a morning person."

"I'll make a note of that."

Jamie waved goodbye, then started up the porch steps as Austin turned and headed away. He let himself in and turned on the lights, sighing like a schoolgirl when he locked the door. It was nearly midnight, he needed to get up for work, and he really should get to sleep. But just to make sure he drifted off smoothly, Jamie figured jerking off to thoughts about Austin would certainly make for pleasant dreams.

3

AUSTIN

The idea of seeing Jamie again made a day of research sound like a great plan to Austin as he drank his morning java from the in-room coffeemaker. He'd been surprised and secretly thrilled when Jamie invited him to dinner last night. Austin usually took the initiative, especially with a younger partner. He wondered if Jamie would be equally forward asking for pleasure, and he certainly hoped he'd get a chance to find out.

It's been a while. My social skills are probably rusty. Then again, the evening had gone smoothly, without the uncomfortable pauses and awkward moments that seemed fated to be part of first dates. *Was that a date? If not, I'm definitely asking him on one tonight.*

Austin had enjoyed their conversation throughout dinner and how natural it felt. It had taken real effort not to stare at Jamie, especially at those light blue eyes that seemed big as saucers, with long, dark lashes. The plush lips gave Austin all kinds of naughty ideas, and he wondered if Jamie had noticed that he'd been half hard all night.

Especially when they'd gone back to the gaming room. Austin loved the look of concentration on Jamie's face when he threw darts and the way he bit his lip as he lined up his shot at the pool table. He wanted Jamie to look at him with that kind of focus. When Jamie bent over to shoot pool, legs wide and jeans taut over that fine ass, Austin needed to adjust himself.

I'd like to bend him over, just like that, and fuck us both sense-less. He'd made quick work of getting off when he went to bed, imagining what Jamie looked like under all those clothes. Dusky nipples, a toned stomach, and a happy trail of dark hair leading to a wiry thatch of curls around what Austin pictured as an ample cock and manscaped balls. He'd come embarrassingly fast and tried to tell himself it had just been due to a long dry spell.

Austin sighed as he remembered last night; then he set his mug aside, stripped off his sleep pants at the bathroom door, and turned on the shower. He soaped up, making quick work of shampooing his hair before his hand fell to his stiff cock. A few long pulls made him even harder, and twisting his palm over the already-leaking head set the mood.

He pictured Jamie naked and horny, bent over with his forearms on the back of the motel couch, ass ready for action. Austin groaned, and his hand sped up, thinking about how he'd take hold of Jamie's hips, line himself up, and press into that tight, perfect hole. He came harder than usual, painting his release on the shower's tile walls.

Damn. I've got it bad. He hadn't planned to find a boyfriend for the duration of his time in Saranac Lake, but he'd take whatever Jamie was offering.

Austin dried himself off and felt a pang of guilt. As attractive a diversion as Jamie presented, he couldn't forget why he came here. Tracking Thomas's disappearance and—he felt certain—murder had to remain his priority.

Given what happened at the library yesterday, Austin wondered how many of the people who played a part in the disappearances might still be in town. If they'd been in their twenties then, they'd be in their mid-seventies by now, so the possibility wasn't far-fetched.

Austin wasn't terribly worried about being jumped in a dark alley by an angry septuagenarian, but people that age still could hold positions of influence, and their adult children might feel protective. He was lucky that Jamie wasn't from the area, or he might have found himself stonewalled like at the library. Blowing the lid off a local scandal wasn't likely to win him the key to the city, especially when Austin bet the rumors had been circulating, unsubstantiated, for decades.

But it might bring peace to the families of those who vanished.

Austin bundled up, grabbed his messenger bag with his computer and notebook, and headed out. He made a point of stopping for coffee like he'd promised, plus a bunch of creamer and sweetener packets since he didn't know how Jamie liked his brew. He grabbed a half-dozen donuts for good measure, figuring they could wash away the sticky glaze before handling any precious old documents.

The crisp breeze nipped his nose, but he didn't have a free hand to adjust his scarf. Austin's thoughts fell to less pleasant matters than he'd had in the shower. Jamie was the same man from Austin's visions, the one he'd seen frightened and in danger. Was Austin putting Jamie at risk asking for his help? He felt pretty sure that the answer was "yes," and that bothered him on more than one level.

He's a good guy. I don't want to cause trouble for him. But I don't see how I can chase my leads without his help. And he seemed genuinely interested in finding answers.

Before he'd come to Saranac Lake and met Jamie, he'd been worried about the stranger in his visions. Now that they had started to get to know each other, Austin realized that concern had deepened and changed. He liked Jamie—probably more than he should after such a brief time. Their quick connection brought out a gut-deep protectiveness that took Austin by surprise.

Guess I need to rein in my inner caveman. I'm quite sure Jamie knows how to take care of himself and wouldn't appreciate getting treated like a damsel in distress.

He wasn't ready to look at why Jamie's safety mattered quite so much or what his subconscious might know that it hadn't shared with the rest of his brain.

Despite the cold wind, both coffees were still hot when Austin reached the Historical Association. He was in the process of trying to wedge the door open with his foot and elbow without dropping the cups when Jamie spotted him and ran to help.

"Let's take this into the kitchen, so we don't have liquids around the old stuff," Jamie said, leading the way once Austin made it through the doorway. He glanced around, assuring himself that no one else had come in.

"I set the door to chime when it opens," Jamie told him. "That way I'll know, in case I'm back in the stacks. If I'll be away from the front desk for more than a few minutes, I can flip the *Back Shortly* sign. I do need to dig something out of storage, and I was waiting for you to arrive. I've got some ideas after our chat last night."

Austin handed Jamie a cup and the bag full of fixings. Jamie took off the lid and inhaled, letting his eyelids flutter shut, lips upturned in bliss. Austin wished he could put that same look on Jamie's face and shifted slightly in his chair as he chubbed up at the thought.

"Thank you," Jamie said. "Sugar and coffee. Perfect for getting a good start on an overcast day." He dumped all of the cream and three of the sweeteners into the oversized cup. Austin held out the bag of donuts, and Jamie pondered for a moment before selecting one with a chocolate iced glaze.

The flecks of sugar that dotted his lips after he took a bite gave Austin one more reason to want to lick them clean.

When they finished, Jamie tossed the empties into the trash, and they both washed away any sticky traces from their hands that might damage old manuscripts.

"I came in a little early to pull some resources," Jamie said and pointed to a big worktable that held two stacks of old books. "We've got some records that the library doesn't —just due to the odd way organizations write their rules," he explained with a shrug. "Anyhow, figured we could start with these. See if there's anything that jumps out."

"We? I don't want to take you away from your work," Austin protested, although he had secretly hoped they could work together.

Jamie smiled. "Making sure the old documents are handled properly is my job. And the work will go quicker with two."

That warmed Austin's heart, but he needed to make sure Jamie realized the possible danger. "The information we might uncover could ruffle feathers," he cautioned. "Some of the people involved could still be alive. I think the real situation is bigger than a handful of patients running away. People get pissy when they feel threatened, and digging up old dirt might not endear you to the townsfolk."

Jamie rolled his eyes. "Temporary job, remember? And if

they were in on the disappearances or helped cover them up, those aren't the kind of people I want to know, anyhow. Count me in." He shot Austin a reckless grin, and Austin felt himself fall a little harder.

The morning passed quickly with both men seated at the worktable, carefully going through the stacks of old records and journals that Jamie had pulled from the back shelves. Occasionally someone stopped in to ask a question or drop off a flyer for the bulletin board. Now and then, Jamie or Austin would get up to stretch and drink a cup of coffee in the break room. The work could have felt like drudgery, but Austin found that working with Jamie made sitting in silence familiar and comfortable.

"There are pages missing," Austin said, looking up mid-afternoon. "How about in yours?"

Jamie closed the book he had been reading and pushed it away. "Yeah. And always in a section about the hospital. Who had time to do all that?"

Austin leaned back. "Who had the job here, before you?"

"Richard Mason. He was the Historical Association director for thirty-some years. Knew everyone, thick as thieves with the 'People in Charge,'" Jamie replied. Austin heard the capital letters without Jamie resorting to finger quotes. "I guess he's the most likely culprit. What do they say in the police shows? It's all about access and motive?"

"What happened to Mason?" Austin needed a mental break. His eyes were already starting to blur from the small type and cramped handwriting.

"Died in his sleep, or so I hear. I don't think he had been doing much work toward the end. They staffed the desk with volunteers for a month until they brought me in. A lot of stuff didn't get done." Jamie suddenly looked up, eyes alight. "I just thought of something. Do you mind watching the door for a little bit?"

"Sure," Austin replied. "What do I do if someone comes in?"

"Find out what they want, help them if you can, and if you can't, have them write down what they need and their phone number," Jamie replied. "It's a pretty quiet gig. We don't get many walk-ins. Most of what I do is work through the backlog of donations and acquisitions that haven't been entered into the catalog. Don't worry—you'll be fine for a few minutes."

Jamie headed down the hallway, and Austin heard him climbing the stairs to the second floor. He went back to the worktable and reminded himself that the chime would let him know if someone opened the door while his attention was elsewhere.

The books Jamie had pulled included binders with the minutes of long-ago town council meetings, self-published autobiographies, and books by area historians, all from around the time Thomas had gone missing. For someone to have gone to all the trouble of removing pages from these books and the ones at the library, Austin figured there had to be something much bigger than one teenager's disappearance.

Austin had his list of missing patients, but he wondered if the truth went far beyond that, both in how long the disappearances continued and how many people were involved. None of the possibilities he imagined were good.

To Austin's relief, no one came in while Jamie was gone. He returned carrying a records storage box, which he thumped down onto the table with a look of triumph.

"Another box?" Austin wasn't sure what made this one so special.

"I think Richard was unwell for a long time before he died. I didn't want to say anything and 'sully his memory' because it didn't really matter, but the place was a mess when I took over. The volunteers just answered the phone and sorted the mail," Jamie said, dropping his voice although there was no one around to hear his uncharitable opinion.

"That meant that any new materials got stuck on the shelves of 'to be cataloged' stuff and forgotten," Jamie went on, a glint of victory in his eyes.

"Like this one?"

Jamie nodded. "It took me a little digging to find the box I wanted. The association had a program called 'Our World Through Their Eyes.' Cool idea—asking for the diaries, letters, and photos of regular people to capture a 'man in the street' view of local history, what they thought was important to remember." He sighed. "Kinda sad that they've never gotten around to doing the exhibit."

"And gathering the boxes continued, even after Richard died?" Austin started to catch on and felt excitement rise.

"It pretty much ran on automatic, at least as far as intake went," Jamie told him. "People could download the instructions from the website, then they filled out a form, packed up their boxes, and dropped them off on Tuesday mornings. Whoever was on duty stuck the boxes on the shelves to be entered into the system."

"Then how did you know this particular box was there?"

"The system created a list every month. When I got here, no one had downloaded it in ages. So I got curious." Jamie slapped his hand down on the top of the box, raising a small cloud of dust. "Steve Ramsey was an orderly at Havenwood, back in the sixties and seventies. No one was paying attention when this came in, so they didn't have a chance to rip out pages."

"What are we waiting for? Let's have a look!" Austin said as Jamie pulled off the lid.

A heap of papers nearly filled the container. Jamie lifted them out carefully, handful by handful. It looked like someone had cleaned off their desk and just swept everything loose into the box. "I guess we're going to have to go through sheet by sheet," Jamie said. "So much for organization."

They divided the yellowing papers between them and began to read. Steve had collected odds and ends about the community, including newspaper clippings, event posters, and photos taken around the area. One large black and white picture caught Austin's attention.

The photo had a group of young men lined up on the steps to a large building, like a class picture. Except that they were all wearing loose, pajama-style tops and pants, and none of them managed a convincing smile for the camera. Austin flipped the print over and squinted to read the faded handwriting on the back.

Havenwood Hospital, June 1965. The list of names were clearly spaced to match with the people on the front. *Thomas McKean.*

Austin looked at the haunted eyes of the boy on the stairs and found himself overwhelmed with emotion. *Whatever went wrong couldn't have been worth sending him away, throwing him out. He didn't get help or treatment—they betrayed him again.*

"Find something?" Jamie asked, and from his quiet voice, Austin knew the other man had probably guessed.

He slid the photo across to Jamie. "That's Thomas," he said, pointing to his great-uncle.

"Shit. They're just kids." Jamie sounded sad and angry.

"And someone took advantage of him," Austin added, feeling his fury surface.

"I didn't find anything quite so dramatic," Jamie said, "But this looks like a duty roster page. Don't know why it's in here, but it gives us some names to research. Maybe these people are still alive."

Austin took a picture of both the photo and the roster with his phone. Nothing else seemed relevant, but Jamie put the box back where he had found it to avoid calling attention to it, in case anyone noticed.

"Ready for dinner?" Austin asked when Jamie returned from the second floor. "I think we accidentally skipped lunch."

Jamie grinned. "Sounds good to me. Want to go back to the Moosehead again, or try something different?"

The promise of playing another round of pool with Jamie was tempting enough, although good food and beer didn't detract. "Why mess with success?" He glanced at the clock and realized that the day had flown. "I know the drill —meet you outside."

Jamie looked oddly spooked again when he came out several minutes later, but maybe a bit less so than last night. Austin figured his friend would tell him what that was all about when he was ready. Not that it mattered, but Austin couldn't help being curious. Then again, Austin wasn't ready to spoil a good thing by confessing his visions, so maybe he could let Jamie have his secrets.

Austin got the Philly cheesesteak this time and tried a different local beer. Jamie ordered a Frisco melt, and they split jalapeño poppers and house made tortilla chips and salsa. Their conversation covered everything from music to vacation spots and felt casual and comfortable. To Austin, it seemed like they'd known each other much longer than a couple of days.

Jamie seemed interested, but he wasn't flirting hard, which Austin appreciated. Even though his time in Saranac Lake was limited, and the attraction that flared between them seemed to grow stronger every day, Austin knew in his gut that this wasn't a one-night stand. Not just because he needed Jamie's help—Austin had started to care about the historian, and he wanted the time they had together to be something special. That was worth taking it slow.

Jamie held his own tonight at pool, while Austin represented himself better at darts. They weren't seriously competing, but Austin felt like he'd salvaged a bit of his honor, and Jamie seemed to be having fun.

"I'm going to see if I can chase down the names on the roster tomorrow," Austin said when he and Jamie had reached the steps to his duplex. "So I won't be at the archive. But if you don't have plans, I'd like to meet up for dinner and drinks again."

He found himself holding his breath. Last night and tonight could just be excused as two colleagues having a convenient meal after work. This felt like a real, planned date.

Jamie gave him a big smile and reached out to rest his hand on Austin's arm, a touch he swore he felt even through the heavy parka. "I'd like that. And maybe afterward, we can come back here for a nightcap. Since no one has to drive." The look in his eyes made Austin plump up his jeans despite the cold.

"That sounds perfect." Austin realized that they were standing very close. Jamie's face tilted up to meet his gaze, and his tongue flicked over those tempting, full lips.

"May I?" he breathed, barely a whisper.

Jamie nodded, eyes open, and stretched up on his toes to bridge the distance between them as Austin slipped an arm around his waist and leaned in to press a kiss against the lips that fueled his fantasies.

It didn't last nearly long enough, but they were on a public street, in the cold, and Austin didn't know how gay-friendly this town might be. He didn't want to find out the hard way. Even so, their kiss surged through him like lightning, right to his groin—and his heart.

"I'll see you tomorrow," he promised, wondering if Jamie's pulse pounded just as fast, unable to see beneath the long parka to know whether his partner's cock was also straining against its zipper.

"Looking forward to it." Jamie sounded breathless and turned on. It took all of Austin's control to let Jamie walk away, up the steps and into his house. He saw the lights go on, and then Jamie looked out the window and waved good-bye. Austin grinned and waved back.

Despite the cold, he found himself whistling as he walked to his motel.

Up ahead, Austin noticed a light on in one of the store-fronts. *That's odd.* It was the middle of the week, not a night stores generally picked for late hours, and it had to be almost midnight. Austin knew he would have noticed if a shop had been open when he walked back last night.

He stopped in front of the store, feeling a curious draw to go inside despite the late hour. The place had an old-school vibe, with a black painted wood facade and two big plate glass windows on either side of the doorway, beneath a dark green awning. Austin had always enjoyed antique and curio stores, feeling like an explorer and never knowing what he might find.

Marden's Magic Emporium was emblazoned in gilt

lettering across the right-hand window. On the left, it read *Marvels. Wonders. Necessities.* Maybe Austin had more beer than he thought, but the doorway actually seemed to *glow*. The store and its entrance looked completely out of place with the rest of Saranac Lake's upscale, outdoor hipster vibe.

Everything about the unlikely shop pinged his investigator instincts, while the part of him that got visions argued for caution. He opened the door and went inside, feeling a frisson of energy that raised the hair on the back of his neck.

"Whoa," he muttered. The interior looked like a cross between a shop from Diagon Alley and one of those pop-up Halloween stores. A large cauldron bubbled in one corner, and purple clouds seemed to be forming their own weather pattern on the ceiling. A life-size mermaid sculpture confronted him, boldly naked to the waist, holding a crystal ball that glowed with an inner fire.

Glittering arrows directed Austin to go around the statue to a solid stone counter that blocked a huge doorway that he guessed led to the rest of the store. The air smelled of citrus and old parchment.

"Hello?" Austin called, wondering who was on duty. He had tried to pay attention to the posters on the local bulletin boards and couldn't remember seeing anything about a costume ball or the kind of event that would send costumers and cosplayers scurrying to outfit themselves at a place like this.

"You're late." A tall, slender man stood up behind the counter. He had long, white-blond hair, milky-pale skin, and —Austin couldn't quite believe his eyes—pointed ears. "You were supposed to be here sooner."

"Yeah well, I'm here now," Austin managed to reply. *I've wandered into some kind of escape room set-up or a bunch of LARPers playing an elaborate game. Maybe the crazy alchemist's shop vibe brings in the stoners and goths. It's pretty cool. The guy is really into his role—gotta love theater majors.*

An old cash box sat on the stone counter, next to a disreputable-looking burlap sack. Austin blinked, and a man appeared behind the strange elf-clerk. The old man wore honest-to-god wizard robes and had long gray hair and a beard. He nodded to the clerk and then regarded Austin with a look that seemed to see down to his bones. It might have been Austin's imagination, but he thought the wizard had a faint tinge of blue beneath his skin, like the dim glow of blacklight. As if he needed help looking like he might actually *be* a mage.

Which is crazy, right?

"What do you want most?" The clerk asked, pulling Austin's attention away from the Gandalf wanna-be. Austin glanced at the "elf," and when he looked back again, the wizard was gone.

"I, uh, don't know. I just saw your sign and came in," Austin said, feeling like reality had started to come unglued. "I don't know what I need."

"I didn't ask what you needed," the clerk replied with a hint of annoyance. "The save-me sack will know what you need. I asked what you *want* most. Say what's on your heart. I don't have all day."

"A safe haven." Austin couldn't believe he'd blurted out what came to mind, but he knew the truth of it as soon as he heard his words. He wanted to do the work he enjoyed around people who valued his skills instead of mistrusting him. He wished for the time to see what might happen between him and Jamie. And he wanted to find answers for his grandmother and the family members of the other missing people so that they could find peace.

The elf nodded. "That's fine. The save-me sack will know what you are in dire need of to make that happen."

Austin raised an eyebrow, but before he could ask, the man in the elf costume picked up the burlap sack. He reached in, rooted around, and withdrew a slip of paper, which he didn't bother to show to Austin.

"Hmmm. Yes. That makes sense," the man murmured. He turned back to Austin. "Come with me. I know where your item is located," he added, holding the paper. "I've got the room, aisle, and bin number right here."

Austin backed up a step and nearly ran into the mermaid. "That's okay. I was just looking."

The elven clerk shook his head. "The sack is never wrong. If your need isn't dire yet—it will be. You'll thank us later. Follow me."

Austin felt a deep compulsion to do as the man suggested. Then again, he was curious about what lay on the other side of the doorway, an area that seemed larger than the storefront should occupy. Going with his gut, Austin stepped around the counter and followed the clerk deeper into the shop.

"You're skeptical," the clerk said. "Ex-cop, private investigator—you're the suspicious type."

"How do you know—"

The elf looked over his shoulder with a smirk. "Magic, remember?"

They passed through a corridor with swords and daggers of every description, age, and size hanging on both walls. Austin lagged, looking at the beautiful workmanship.

"Don't touch." The clerk didn't even look back at him. Austin let his hand fall back to his side from where he had just barely started to reach out.

"Are those real?"

The clerk spared him a look over one shoulder. "Do we look like the kind of place that sells *fake* swords?"

Austin swallowed hard, wondering if someone had slipped something in his drink at the bar, but everything had seemed perfectly normal until he came into the strange shop.

From the corridor of swords they turned down a wide hallway that stretched as far as Austin could see, with doors on both sides every few feet. The clerk glanced at the slip of paper once more. "This way."

He selected a door and opened it, leading into a large storeroom. Tall wooden shelves stretched from floor to ceiling, filled with all kinds of bottles, tins, vials, crates, and boxes. Ruby-colored banners hung over the ends of each row and streamed down from the ceiling in random places.

Those TV shows about hoarders would have a lot of fun with this place, Austin thought as he followed the elf.

"The item you need should be right over there," the clerk said, as Austin craned his neck, turning from side to side to glimpse the unusual and disturbing items on the shelves.

"What *is* this place?" Austin wondered aloud.

"Marden's Magic Emporium," the clerk answered in a dead-pan voice. "Did you not read the sign before you entered?"

Austin stared at the back of the man's head, looking for the seam where the fake pointed ear extensions were attached, but either the clerk had Hollywood-quality makeup, or...

He can't be a real elf...can he?

Is that really so different from getting visions?

Austin's visions had always showed him true glimpses of

things he couldn't otherwise know, and he had seen enough strange occurrences to believe in ghosts.

But elves? And does that mean the guy in the robe is...

"Here we are." The clerk searched up and down in a section of shelves, then held the note in his hand against a label on the shelf to verify. An unremarkable wooden box sat on the shelf, between a large glass jar holding questionable contents afloat in strange green liquid and what appeared to be a taxidermied ferret with horns.

"Very well," the elf said, picking up the wooden box gingerly as if afraid it—or its contents—might bite. "Follow me. We'll get you checked out, and you can be on your way."

"Aren't you going to open it?" Austin felt a little cheated after the big build-up.

The clerk raised an eyebrow. "You may do so at the counter once it's paid for. I wouldn't presume to open it. And the box might prefer that only the rightful owner have the honor. Best not to annoy the box."

Annoy the box? "How much is it?" Austin demanded.

"I'll know when I ring you up—at the front." The clerk sounded like Austin was slow on the uptake.

Austin figured that arguing would be pointless, and the sooner he got back to the front, the sooner he could escape this odd little break from reality. Still, he wondered what the magic sack thought he might be in dire need of and what that had to do—if anything—with the elf asking to know what Austin truly wanted.

"Suit yourself," Austin muttered.

Since the aisles between the rows of shelves were too narrow for the two of them to switch places, Austin led the way back to the shop entrance. The wizard was gone, but everything else was just as weird and fantastical as before.

The elf put the wooden box on the counter next to the

floppy sack, peered at it intensely, then stood. "That will be fifteen dollars," he announced, although Austin didn't see any markings or stickers with a price.

Fifteen, his mind supplied. *The same as Thomas's age when he went missing.* The similarity seemed more like a coincidence than an omen, but Austin felt suddenly uneasy. He handed over the cash and realized he was holding his breath.

Once the elf put the money in the cash box, he pushed the wooden chest toward Austin. "It's yours now. Have a look."

Austin turned the box to face him and released the bronze hook from its clasp. The clerk braced himself as though something might leap out. Austin tensed, expecting danger, then gently lifted the lid, making sure to stand at arm's length.

Nothing burst loose, no strange vapors wafted free, not even a flash of fire or a clap of thunder. Austin moved closer cautiously and looked inside. A yellowed piece of paper the size of an index card lay on the faded blue silk lining the interior of the box.

Austin removed the paper gingerly, fearing it might crumble to dust or burst into flame. It did neither. He studied it closely, first one side and then the other. The paper was blank except for a row of six digits.

I didn't think it was going to be the meaning of life, but all this over a number?

"Hmm," the clerk said, peering at the paper. "How...curious."

"What am I supposed to do with it?" Austin stared at the paper as if it might bite.

"That's not for me to know," the clerk replied. "But since the save-me sack is never wrong, you will have dire need of the note. I would suggest putting it in a safe place."

Austin gently folded the paper to fit in his wallet and found a place where it wasn't likely to fall out. Fifteen dollars for a half-dozen numbers? He couldn't help the feeling that this was all an elaborate prank for a reality TV show whose emcee would jump out at any minute to make fun of his gullibility. When that didn't happen, Austin felt a little sheepish at the clerk's curious expression.

"That's it? I just hold onto this paper until it comes in handy?"

The elf rolled his eyes. "You'll know when the time is right. Dire need, remember?"

"Thanks, I guess," Austin said as the clerk moved to stand behind the counter. "See you around."

"Oh, I strongly doubt that," the other man said with a smirk. "Have a good evening."

Walking out the door meant passing through the same strange energy that made Austin shiver and raised the hair on the back of his arms. He patted his wallet to assure himself that it was in his pocket and resisted the urge to look back at the shop.

Just keep walking. Nothing good ever comes from looking back.

Austin made it to the motel in record time, managing a brisk pace despite how the cold air made his lungs ache. He locked the door and leaned against it, trying to catch his breath, knowing that his shivering wasn't just from the temperature.

What the everlasting fuck just happened?

He pulled out his wallet, fearing that the paper would be gone, a figment of his imagination. But there it was, right where he had put it. Solid and real.

I didn't feel unsafe, Austin thought, turning his investigator's talents to explain his strange experience. *But I did feel like I'd stepped into another world, someplace that isn't really supposed to be here. That was cool...and creepy. Tomorrow, I'm going back to see what it's like in daylight. I'm sure there's a rational explanation.*

Because if there isn't, I've just gone through the looking glass, and that sort of thing never goes well.

4

JAMIE

"Well, hi there. Nice to see you again. We met at the get-acquainted reception the historical association put on when you were hired. I'm Carol, if you didn't remember." The older woman at the county records office offered a broad smile and a warm hand to shake.

"Good to see you too," Jamie replied, although he had met so many people that night, the faces were all a blur.

"What can I do for you?" Carol took a sip of her tea, and even at a distance, Jamie could smell the honey and lemon.

"Working on an article for the newsletter," Jamie replied, figuring that was safer than anything close to the truth. "Just need to go riffle through some old records, if that's okay."

"Knock yourself out," Carol replied with a vague gesture toward the stairs that led to the records archive. "It's all labeled, and there's a guidebook if you need it. If you get stumped, just ask—I'm sure I can help you find it."

Jamie grinned. "I'll be fine—poking around library stacks is second nature by now."

He hurried to the staircase before she could change her

mind. The records office opened earlier than the Historical Association, so Jamie figured he could take a quick look and still have time to pick up coffee on the way. No one ever stopped by the archive this early, but Jamie didn't want this to be the one time his boss chose to drop in for a chat.

Jamie hadn't been to this records room before, but he'd seen dozens like it. Thanks to library science, they all worked the same way—or they were supposed to, if everyone followed the rules. He went straight for the police reports and breathed a sigh of relief when he found the volume for 1965.

The public library had copies, intended to cut down on the traffic at the records office, but these were the real documents, and Jamie hoped they hadn't been tampered with. Damaging the library versions was vandalism, but altering the official copies broke laws.

He worked quickly, taking pictures with his phone instead of diving into the details right then. Jamie paged through the missing persons reports for the entire year, snapping photos of any that had not been resolved. He figured he and Austin could sort them out later.

For a town the size of Saranac Lake, the number of people who went missing seemed high. He didn't doubt that teenagers decided to catch a bus to the big city or that frustrated middle-aged men got wanderlust. Still, one thing that stood out even in Jamie's hurry was that the majority were between fifteen and twenty-five years old, and nearly all were listed as patients at Havenwood Hospital.

The alarm on his phone reminded him that he was out of time. Reluctantly, Jamie replaced the binder and headed back upstairs. "Thanks, Carol. Have a great day."

"Find what you needed?"

"I think so. If not, I'll be back."

"Bring donuts. The way to my heart is through my stomach," she said with a laugh.

Jamie slipped into line at Sunrise Coffee, a mom-and-pop breakfast shop that had been around long enough to be a local favorite. The queue didn't surprise him since the coffee was good enough to be worth it, even without friendly baristas who remembered everyone's names and the comfortable feeling of eating in a family kitchen. Their offerings certainly beat what he brewed at the association.

He glanced around the room at the diners while he waited, recognizing some by face if not by name. Two older men at one of the tables caught his attention just as the barista handed Jamie his order. Before he could second-guess himself, Jamie took his cup and walked over.

"Good morning, Mr. Quincey," he greeted a man he recognized from the Historical Association. Benjamin Quincey was an amateur historian, a retired history teacher, and a willing volunteer at community events both at the library and the archive. Jamie figured the man had to be in his late seventies, old enough that he might have some helpful memories about the missing people.

"Well hello, Jamie. Nice to see you. Treating yourself to some good coffee before the workday?" Quincey asked.

"Yes, sir," Jamie replied. "Coffee makes everything better," he added with a conspiratorial wink.

"You're welcome to join us if you have a moment," Quincey said. "This is Pete Lawson, and Ed Thompson just went to the men's room, but he'll be back." He turned to Pete. "This is Jamie Miller, the one who's filling in at the Historical Association 'til they find a permanent replacement for Richard."

Pete gave a curt nod and went back to his newspaper and

his Danish. That made Jamie bold enough to ask his question.

"I'm working on an article for the website—it's the 150th anniversary of the old Havenwood Hospital. And as I was pulling odds and ends together, I found comments about people going missing. Not that I'd ever put something like that in the article," Jamie made sure to say, "but just for myself, I was wondering—is any of that true?"

Pete shrugged. "Never paid much attention to that place," he mumbled and turned back to his paper.

Quincey frowned, hesitating for a moment before he spoke. "I wouldn't want to be quoted—"

"Never. I promise."

"I didn't work at Havenwood, but I had friends and neighbors who did. They came home with plenty of tales about what happened. Gotta understand, it was a long time ago. We think about a lot of things differently now. And the people who were there—they weren't quite right, if you know what I mean."

"Mentally ill?" Jamie supplied.

An expression of discomfort flashed across Quincey's face. "Some were. Others I think were just odd, didn't know how to act like people expected them to, and didn't have anyone who cared enough to teach 'em, I guess. And it didn't help when the witch rumors went around."

Pete roused from his paper and gave Quincey a warning look. "Some things are best forgotten."

"Witch rumors?" Jamie asked, a little breathless.

"The place is closed, and most of the folks from back then are dead. It's just old stories now," Quincey told Pete, who muttered something Jamie didn't catch and turned back to his paper.

"Someone new would come in from time to time who

might have been odder than most, I guess, and the story would go around that they were a witch or had some sort of magic," Quincey said. "People like to talk, and we couldn't play on our phones the way folks do now," he added with a deeply creased smile. "Anyhow, never was anything to it, except tall tales that got bigger every time they were passed along. And then if one of the 'witch' patients went missing, people spun all kinds of reasons why."

"What do you think happened to the patients who disappeared?" Jamie asked.

"Always figured they got loose and wandered off. There are a lot of woods around here. Easy to get lost, hard to be found. 'Specially for someone who might not be firing on all cylinders, if you know what I mean."

"Why do you need to know about that?" The harsh voice came from behind Jamie, and he jumped, not realizing the third member of the group had returned.

"Settle down, Ed," Quincey said. Jamie half-turned in his seat to find a short, broad-shouldered man with white hair and a thunderous expression looming over him. "We're just swapping stories."

"We don't need anyone raking up old dirt," Ed continued, ignoring Quincey and fixing Jamie with a glare. "Whatever happened back then is long over. Leave it be, and good riddance." His sharp tone and the sudden anger in his eyes made Jamie shift away from him.

"Of course," Jamie agreed quickly, not wanting a confrontation. "Sometimes I get so caught up in the old stories I just forget—"

"Well, stop. Do your job, and don't go poking your nose where it doesn't belong," Ed snapped, moving to sit down as Jamie scurried out of the way, nearly spilling his coffee in his hurry to get up from the table.

"Sorry to bother you. Thanks, Mr. Quincey. Hope you all have a nice day," Jamie said, talking a little too quickly as he backed away and almost tripped a server. He swore he could feel Ed's gaze follow him until he was safely out the door and down the street.

I kicked a hornet's nest with that one. He watched the steam rise from his coffee in the cold air.

But what if there was *something to those "witch" rumors? People might look at me funny if I talked about seeing ghosts, but nowadays, they wouldn't lock me away. Same with the people who do psychic readings and are actually good at it. But back in the day, if you could do those things and someone found out, they might think you were nuts. Send you to a place like Havenwood...*

The longer Jamie thought about it, the more he became convinced that he'd stumbled onto an important clue. Whether Austin would believe him was another matter.

―――

THE MORNING PASSED QUICKLY as Jamie worked hard to clear away tasks related to his actual job so he could focus on finding new information for Austin. The historical association usually only had one employee—the director—and brought in volunteers for special events, like the annual fundraiser. Before computers and answering machines, Jamie suspected they had also retained a secretary, but technology had sidelined that job long ago.

Since he was alone, Jamie listened to his favorite playlist of smooth jazz as he reshelved books, paid bills, and handled the mail. A cleaning person came once a week to vacuum and dust, so at least he didn't have to worry about that. Five books he had ordered for the collection had arrived, and he entered them into the system. Nothing took his full attention, which left his mind free to wonder if he had overlooked any other useful resources in the materials that hadn't been cataloged.

By now it was past lunch with no walk-in visitors, so Jamie didn't feel guilty about flipping the sign at the front window to *Back in an Hour* and locking the door. He left all the lights on so no one would think he had closed for the day and headed upstairs.

A cold spot made him shiver, and he heard footsteps in the attic, although he knew no one else was in the building. Sometimes the ghosts liked to remind him they were here first, and as long as nothing unfriendly happened, Jamie couldn't begrudge them their claim.

"I'm not here to bother you," he said aloud. "I'm just looking for some information." Jamie paused, realizing that since he had never actually seen the ghosts clearly—most only by their actions, not their form—he had just assumed they were from the same time period as the house.

But what if they aren't? The house might have been other things before it became the association, and people would have lived here until then. It's a long shot, but if any of the ghosts remember the disappearances, maybe they can help.

Jamie didn't like to draw attention to his ability to see and sense ghosts, and it certainly hadn't been something he mentioned on his resume. Even though he was alone in the building, it still required mustering his courage to address the ghosts out loud.

"I don't know if you can help me, but I'd really appreciate it if you could," he began hating how nervous he sounded. "We think someone at Havenwood Hospital was hurting patients—making them disappear. We're trying to find out what happened so their families can be at peace. If you can help, I'd be grateful."

Nothing stirred, and Jamie sighed, reminding himself that it had been an unlikely gamble. He knew he couldn't stay upstairs long enough to go through all of the donated boxes of historical items, but he could sneak away for an hour a day and just say he was going through the boxes for the exhibit that no one had cataloged in case his boss asked. Since it didn't seem like anyone had altered the boxes so far, he hesitated to take them downstairs and possibly draw the wrong attention to them.

He set his phone alarm because Jamie knew that he'd lose track of time. Going through the boxes was like opening presents on Christmas morning—full of all kinds of surprises. As a historian, he knew that what regular people found important often differed dramatically from the headlines, but it still amazed him to see the proof of it in the boxes. Jamie didn't know if he would be at the archive long enough to bring the first phase of the exhibit to life, but he hoped that someone would.

The time passed quickly, and while Jamie found plenty of interesting items, very little was connected to Havenwood. *Maybe I shouldn't be surprised. Working there probably wasn't pleasant, and there were confidentially rules to keep them from talking about patients. But I'd still hoped...*

He put the box back on the shelf and stood. An over-sized portfolio fell from one of the upper shelves, just as Jamie felt as if someone had dropped an ice cube down his back. He stared at the shelf where the folio came from, knowing that he hadn't jostled the bookcase.

Jamie picked up the portfolio and opened it. Inside were floor plans of Havenwood, complete with additions and renovations over the years.

"Thank you," he whispered and knew the spirits were listening.

―――――

"I THOUGHT we'd do something a little different if that's okay," Austin said when he met Jamie after the archive closed. "I'd like to check out the bar at Hotel Saranac."

"Sure," Jamie agreed, noting that Austin looked like he'd dressed up a bit more than usual, more like Jamie's own business casual. "I haven't been there in a while." He hoped this meant they were counting the evening as a real date.

They kept the conversation light all through the meal, and Austin had requested a booth that afforded some privacy, all the way in the back corner where they were unlikely to be overheard. Jamie flirted, laughing and joking, occasionally touching Austin's hand to make a point, holding eye contact just a few seconds too long. Austin's interest was clear in his eyes, even if his attempts to flirt back were endearingly flustered.

I'm out of practice, and maybe he is too. I'm definitely gun shy after the way Curt stomped out. There hasn't been anyone worth the risk since then.

When the dishes were cleared and they lingered over coffee, Jamie told him about the floor plans.

"The folio shouldn't have been on the high shelf." Jamie leaned forward so only Austin could hear him in the buzz of conversations around them. "That isn't where it belonged. I think someone deliberately misfiled it to make it hard to find."

"Maybe the historian in Richard couldn't bear destroying the plans, so he hid them instead," Austin mused.

"I thought they might come in handy," Jamie replied. "I want to photograph them and put them back where they were. We might need them." Jamie had already figured they were going to end up sneaking around the old hospital sooner or later.

"And I think I might have picked up a clue, but I'm not sure how it relates," Jamie added, wondering whether Quincey's odd comment was too weird to mention. "I talked to one of the retired guys who volunteers sometimes at the archive when I went to get coffee this morning. He was there with a couple of his friends, and since they're the right age, I asked if they remembered hearing about the disappearances."

"Did they?"

"One of them, Quincey, did. Just gossip he remembered from family and friends, but he said that sometimes a new patient would get a reputation for being 'witchy.' That's when his other friends started trying to shut him up, and one of them got downright scary."

Austin raised an eyebrow. "Witchy?"

"Quincey said that looking back, he doubts all the patients were mentally ill. He thinks some of them were just eccentric or awkward—things we might call 'behavior problems' now. Which got me wondering—what if someone back then actually was a psychic or a medium and maybe they had just discovered what they could do so they didn't have much control, and someone found out about them..."

Austin met his gaze, and his eyes widened as understanding hit. "Shit. People would say they were crazy. Or they'd get sent off because their abilities scared people who thought it had something to do with the devil."

Jamie nodded. "Can you find out whether there was anything 'unusual' about the missing relatives before they went away?"

Austin leaned back in his chair. "I already asked if the family members knew what caused their relative to be taken away. They didn't—and other relatives refused to talk about it. In a couple of cases, they were children, and the person sent away was a teenager, so they could only give a child's perspective. Or the younger relative was sent off while the older one was away at school or in the military. If they eventually found documents when their parents passed on, they gave them to me, but the paperwork is so vague it's useless," he said, frustrated.

"I know it's a long shot, but I can't help thinking that there might be a connection," Jamie confided. "Although it doesn't answer why they disappeared—or where they went."

Austin fiddled with his coffee spoon. Jamie noticed how his lips pressed together in a firm line, jaw clenched, and his eyebrows drew together like he was deep in thought.

The witchy idea either has him upset or uncomfortable. Maybe it's a good thing I didn't tell him I see ghosts.

"Earth to Austin," Jamie teased, keeping his tone light. "What are you thinking?"

Austin shook himself as if he hadn't meant to get lost in his thoughts. "Sorry. The supernatural angle complicates things. If the patients didn't escape on their own, I was thinking that maybe the able-bodied ones had been 'loaned' out for labor—off the books. That sort of thing wasn't uncommon for prisoners back in the day, and the old mental hospitals usually ran their own farms and carpentry shops, thought it was good 'therapy.'"

"So free illegal workers they just 'forgot' to give back?" Jamie asked, feeling a surge of anger at the idea.

Austin shrugged. "That sort of thing happened elsewhere." He tapped his fingers on the table, quiet for another moment. "But if they thought the patients had extra abilities, that doesn't bode well...especially if there were staff members who were super-religious."

Jamie sighed. "There are a lot of questions and not enough answers yet. Sorry for making it more complicated."

"No, don't apologize," Austin said, shaking his head. "I have a hunch you're on to something. We just haven't connected the dots yet."

Jamie finished his coffee and waved the server away when he started back to refill their cups. "How about you? How did your day go?

"I spent the day trying to locate the people on that duty roster," Austin replied, finishing off his drink. "Two are dead, one moved to Florida, and the others are still in the area. I did some background checks so I know who I'm dealing with. Tomorrow I'll see which ones I can catch in person and whether they'll talk to me."

"Be careful," Jamie warned. "Even if this was the kind of thing everyone knew about and no one ever mentioned, I got the feeling from the grouchy old guy at the coffee shop that folks won't take kindly to bringing it up again."

Austin shot him a devil-may-care smile. "I'm used to people who don't want to answer questions. Eventually, someone will."

Jamie guessed that Austin's job as a private investigator meant dealing with this sort of thing all the time. Grumpy witnesses might be routine for Austin, but Jamie's focus on the Victorian era had led him to think of history as something static, a story about people who were long dead. When research turned up new details, people were interested, not threatened. He'd never had to deal with the impact of past deeds on living people who might have good reason to fear consequences.

History had never seemed dangerous before. Jamie

couldn't deny that excitement buzzed through him like he had landed a part in a suspense thriller.

"Ready to go for a nightcap?" Jamie asked as they paid the bill.

Austin's warm smile was full of promise. "Sounds like a great idea. Lead the way, and I'll follow."

Jamie couldn't help thinking about Austin's words on the way to his apartment. *Did he mean more by that than just the walk home? Like he's waiting for me to set the pace, move us forward from what we are now to...something new?*

Much as Jamie wanted to see how his jerk-off fantasies compared to the real thing, he knew that moving slow made more sense. Even if their fling was limited to the short time both of them would be in Saranac Lake, Jamie wanted to savor every minute. Austin deserved that.

"Well, here we are," Jamie said as he unlocked the door to his duplex, and Austin followed him inside. "The appliances are new-ish, the paint's fairly fresh, and the heat works. It came furnished, so you won't be able to deduce anything about me from the plaid couch or the ugly recliner. I think it's a seasonal rental that belongs to one of the archive's board members. Living here was part of my contract, so I'm not going to complain."

Austin held up both hands palm out in surrender. "Not saying a word. This looks like a palace compared to some of my old apartments."

They hung their coats on hooks by the door, and Jamie went into the kitchen to grab two glasses and his best whiskey. "So what's it like—your place in Albany?"

He knew he shouldn't ask, and he didn't mean to imply that there'd be an "after" for them once the case here was done, that he'd road trip to the state capitol to visit. But Jamie couldn't help being curious.

"When Grandma Helen went into assisted living, she refused to admit that she wouldn't be coming back to the house. So she asked me to stay there—rent free—and keep an eye on the place, feed her cats, 'until she came home.'" Austin's brown eyes grew sad, and he looked away.

"That was three years ago. At the time, it was a godsend because I'd just moved out of the apartment I shared with... someone. I needed a place, and she needed plausible deniability. I can't redecorate because it's her house."

"You have cats?"

"Not anymore," Austin replied. "They were all up in years, and one by one, they went to the big litter box in the sky. But yeah, for a while. I got used to them, and it feels strange without them. God, some of those cats had been around for more than half my life."

"Sorry for your loss," Jamie replied, pouring them each a few fingers of amber liquid. The highland single malt was something he had learned to appreciate in graduate school, and its taste brought back memories from that time. "I've always wanted to get a pet—cat or dog—but even at the grand old age of thirty, I haven't managed to be quite settled enough. Someday." He tried not to sound as wistful as he felt at the thought.

"You're talking to a man who lives in a borrowed house with flowered granny-curtains," Austin said. "I'm not going to judge." He paused to swirl the whiskey in his glass and sniffed the contents. "Damn. You brought out the good stuff."

Jamie chuckled. "It deserves fine crystal, but all I've got are regular water glasses. It's a step up from plastic, which is what we used in my grad school days."

"Cheers," Austin said, raising their glasses to clink together.

They settled on the couch, and Jamie felt hopeful as Austin sat close but not quite touching, a distance that could be easily spanned if desired. They debated movie choices and settled on an old favorite, an action-adventure flick with plenty of explosions they had both seen multiple times. It offered a way to bridge any awkward silences while not demanding their attention.

"Did you notice a new store open up in the next block?" Austin asked as he sipped his drink. "Odd place. Lots of...atmosphere."

Jamie shook his head. "No—but then again, I haven't had time to do much shopping since I got here. Why?"

Austin hesitated, and Jamie wondered what made him look uncomfortable. "Nothing, really. It just didn't seem to fit the outdoors-upscale-hipster or old-money-skier vibe."

Jamie had the feeling Austin had left something out, but it didn't seem important right now to press for details. If it mattered, he figured the other man would tell him, sooner or later.

The whiskey warmed Jamie and loosened the tension in his shoulders. Austin also looked more relaxed, and the longer the movie went on, the more Austin slowly sprawled closer until they were pressed together from knee to hip. A few moments later, Austin slid his arm across the back of the couch, letting gravity gradually settle it over Jamie's shoulders.

Jamie shifted closer, doing his best to signal interest. During the movie's big fight scene, his hand slipped onto Austin's thigh. Austin's thumb started to gently rub Jamie's shoulder, stroking the sensitive skin at the base of his neck. Jamie leaned into the touch and slid his hand higher on Austin's thigh, nearly at the 'V' of his groin.

Austin's fingers tangled with Jamie's hair, gently

massaging his scalp. A light tug went right to Jamie's cock, which was chubbing up quickly. A glance at Austin's crotch assured Jamie that the lust was mutual.

Jamie turned, shifting so he was facing Austin, TV forgotten. He kept one hand on Austin's leg, and he gently cupped his face with the other. "I want to kiss you."

"Then do it."

Jamie moved in slowly, in case Austin changed his mind. He kissed him gently at first, a brush of dry, closed lips, just enough connection to feel his heart speed up and his cock go rock hard.

This close, he could smell Austin's shampoo and soap—rosemary and mint—and a faint trace of cedar and patchouli from his aftershave. Jamie moved even closer, then took a risk and shifted to straddle Austin's lap, which removed all doubt that his partner was equally aroused.

Austin brought his hands up to rest on Jamie's hips, and Jamie changed the angle of the kiss, licking along the seam of Austin's lips, asking to be allowed inside. Austin opened to him, and the kiss changed from tentative and exploring to hungry and claiming. Jamie could taste the whiskey on Austin's tongue, caught the scent on his breath.

If this was all they did tonight, Jamie could be content. Austin pulled him tight, and the slight change lined up their cocks, pressing against each other with delicious friction. Jamie ground his hips down and rocked them together, drawing a quiet moan from his partner.

"What do you want?" Jamie asked, surprised to find himself taking the lead.

"Want to touch you." Austin's voice had dropped to a low, gravelly rumble that stoked the fire in Jamie's groin. "Want you to touch me."

Jamie met his gaze and slid one hand down Austin's

shirt, working the buttons open as he went, loving the way it made Austin's breath hitch. He pushed the halves of the shirt open and traced a finger from the hollow of Austin's throat down over his breastbone, over the thin cotton of his T-shirt, then splayed his fingers, brushing against the hardened nipples already pebbled beneath the fabric.

"Like this?" Jamie asked, his voice silky, his smile seductive.

"Uh-huh. Just like that."

They hadn't had enough whiskey for either of them to get drunk, but Austin's voice sounded a little slurred, and his pupils were wide and dark.

Jamie ducked his head and traced the tendon in the side of Austin's neck with the tip of his tongue. Austin's fingers slipped below the edge of Jamie's shirt, then he inched the flat of his hand across Jamie's abs, skimming over his skin, plucking at his nipples, and rolling them between his thumb and forefinger.

Jamie arched back, trembling. His hips moved on their own accord, chasing pleasure for both of them. Austin matched his movements, then stilled.

"What—"

"Shh," Austin said with a reassuring smile. He reached for Jamie's belt buckle. "This okay?"

Jamie nodded, desperate for more.

Austin fumbled the button and cursed under his breath before slipping it free on the next try. Jamie was already working his partner's jeans open, wriggling his hand inside to stroke Austin's thick erection through the dark fabric underneath, already wet from his leaking dick.

Austin closed his hand around Jamie's cock, letting the pre-come slick his palm. Jamie groaned and pushed down his partner's waistband until he could do the same.

"Let me," Austin said, nudging Jamie's hand away until he could grip both of their cocks, letting them slide against each other, steel beneath velvet.

"God, Austin," Jamie groaned, adding his hand to Austin's so they could encircle them both.

"Just like that," Austin murmured as he tightened his grip and stroked faster.

Jamie felt the heat rising from the base of his spine, and he knew Austin wasn't far behind from the way he panted and moaned.

His climax roared through him, and hot ropes of come fountained over their joined hands seconds before Austin's orgasm claimed him as well, mingling their seed and spattering them both with their release.

Jamie leaned forward, resting their foreheads together, then Austin shifted to kiss him warm and slow, a gentle affirmation.

"That was really good," Austin murmured.

"Mmmm-hmmm," Jamie managed, still lost in a post-climax buzz. He managed to collect his wits a moment later and gave Austin a quick peck on the lips. "I'll be right back," he promised before getting up and heading to the bathroom.

Jamie wiped up and tucked himself back together, then brought a fresh, warm washcloth to take care of Austin, who looked surprised and pleased at the gesture. He tossed the used cloth toward the hallway and settled back beside Austin on the couch as the movie's sequel began to play.

"Can you stay?" Jamie asked. He tried to sound casual but found himself hoping.

Austin kissed the top of his head. "Next time. I didn't bring a bag. But thanks."

Jamie focused on the "next time" and tried not to feel

disappointed. "That works." He let his head rest on Austin's shoulder, and Austin tightened his grip a little, pulling him close.

This is better than "nice." I could get used to this. That's dangerous since neither of us are planning on staying in town, and I think I could fall for him way too easily. So I'll take what I can get, while I can get it, and use the memories to keep me warm after he's gone. After all, Albany's not that far away...

5

AUSTIN

The odd store had vanished.

When Austin left Jamie's house, he walked to his motel, following the same route that had taken him past the Magic Emporium the night before. The old storefront was vacant, with a faded *For Sale* sign on the door. He walked around the block to see the building from all angles, confirming that a store of the size he encountered couldn't have possibly been in that space. Looking through the dirty windowpane, Austin saw an empty shell—no marble counter, no bubbling cauldron, and definitely no life-size mermaid statue. Nothing but dust, a few empty boxes, and scattered trash, like whoever had helped the long-ago occupant move hadn't bothered with a final sweep.

"That's impossible," he muttered and pulled his wallet out, checking to make certain that the paper hadn't disappeared as well.

The mysterious note was right where he'd put it, solid and real. Seeing it in daylight, Austin realized that the paper was high-quality stationery, brown with age. The numbers looked like they were written with a fountain pen, blue ink faded with age, in an old-fashioned style of handwriting. Those details just made the whole thing even stranger.

There's no way someone set that store up for just one day and took it apart again. Too much damn stuff, for one thing. Enough dust that it looked like it had been empty for years. And the store I walked into doesn't look like it would fit in the empty space on the other side of that window.

What the fuck?

Austin had visions, so he wasn't hypocritical enough to doubt the existence of the supernatural. Stories he'd heard from an investigator he knew in Pittsburgh about demons and other creatures made for great nightmare fodder. He could believe there were people—and beings—out there with strange abilities. But he'd always stopped just shy of accepting that magic was real.

Maybe I need to re-think that.

He wished he could write off the Emporium as just another kind of vision, but unless his psychic abilities had spontaneously learned how to drop him into a 3-D virtual reality as solid and real as the Holodeck, Austin didn't see a choice.

Holy shit. But...why me? Why would the store appear for me? Or did other people see it too? The clerk said I was there because I had a "dire need" for something—the numbers. I haven't needed it yet, so that must be in the future?

So the store isn't just magic—it's either psychic or it time-travels?

He spotted a donut shop a few doors down and went inside. The red-and-white decor gave it a retro feel. No cauldrons, mermaids, or elves. Austin waited in line and ordered a coffee and a Boston cream. When the woman at the register rang up his purchase, Austin smiled. "How long ago did the store up the block go out of business?"

She gave him a blank look and then yelled over her shoulder. "Hey, Frank! When did Garinger's go out? Been what, two years?"

"Three," a man's voice called from the other room. "Why? Someone want to buy it?"

She turned back to Austin. "Well?"

He grabbed his coffee and donut. "Just scouting possibilities for now. Thanks."

Outside, Austin felt a chill that he couldn't blame on the difference between the overly warm bakery and the cold Adirondack wind.

Magic might be real.

The thought made his head spin. He turned his imagination to what the numbers might mean. *Six numbers. Not enough to be coordinates. A street number? Maybe a password? A post office box? The last six digits of a Social Security number or a phone number?* The numbers weren't grouped or separated, so he had no way to know if they were a single unit or a sequence.

Without context, the numbers are useless. I can't even start trying to trace them until I can narrow down what they're for. I hope I figure it out before I end up in the "dire need" the elf predicted.

Elf. A real fuckin' Legolas-style elf. I must be losing my mind.

Austin knew he needed to stay focused on the case. The old duty roster from Havenwood wasn't much to go on, but maybe it would open other doors. Then again, other than having worked for the psychiatric hospital, there wasn't anything connecting the box's owner to the disappearances. If workers at the hospital had either been helping patients escape or kidnapping them, Austin doubted the details were widely known, although if it went on long enough, rumors were likely.

All he could do was chase the leads and hope he found a trail of breadcrumbs leading him to a piece of crucial information. Just like any other case, except this time, it was personal.

Six names were on the list, plus that of the dead man who donated the box. Of those, two had also passed away, and one was in Florida. Austin had spent most of the previous day using his internet search skills to dig into all of the former employees, as well as adding what he could find from a few specialized databases.

Aside from working at Havenwood and living in Saranac Lake, the people had little in common. Their tenures overlapped, with some having started long before the year Thomas disappeared, and others who had been new hires at the time continuing to work there long after.

Nothing in Austin's searches turned up red flags. No criminal records—other than a few speeding tickets—no licensing violations or disciplinary actions, nothing in any federal database to suggest they'd been considered dangerous. It didn't give him much to work with, but Austin knew that cases could sometimes blow wide open in the most unlikely ways.

He headed for the first person on his list, Jonah Neeson, age seventy-six, a retired orderly. *Widowed, two grown children, retired ten years ago. No unusual affiliations.*

The small house looked snug and well-maintained, Austin thought as he climbed the steps to the front porch and rang the bell. An older man opened the door just enough to see him.

"Whatever you're selling, I don't want it. I don't go to church, don't need a lawn service, and I'm not planning on a new roof." He started to shut the door.

"Mr. Neeson—wait. I'm not selling anything. I'm

working on an article about Havenwood Hospital, and I wanted to ask you what it was like back in the day."

Neeson paused, glaring at him through the one-inch gap. "What it was like? Hell on earth. We did the best we could, but those folks—they deserved better. Can't change it, so what's the point of bringing it up?"

"Did you know Thomas McKean? He was a patient who disappeared in 1965."

The one eye that Austin could see narrowed with mistrust. "That was a long time ago. You oughta let the dead stay buried."

"Did he die?" Austin pressed. "Because technically he's still just 'missing.'"

Austin didn't need to see the man's whole face to know Neeson was scowling. "That's a figure of speech. I don't remember what happened that long ago—hell, I barely remember what I had for breakfast. Now get off my porch before I call the cops."

The door slammed shut.

Can't say I expected much else, Austin thought as he headed for his car. He wondered about the comment. *Did Neeson know more than he admitted? Or did he just not want to get involved?*

He pulled out his phone as he started the car and texted Jamie.

Austin: *Struck out on Interview #1. Wish me luck with #2.*

By the time Austin reached the stop sign at the end of the next street, he had a reply.

Jamie: *Went through another couple of "Through Their Eyes" boxes. Didn't find anything useful. But there are more, so maybe we'll get lucky.*

Austin chuckled as he typed a response.

Austin: *I can help you get lucky.*

Jamie: *I'm counting on it.*

His next stop was at a tidy, one-story cottage in a senior community. Ron Wade was seventy-eight, divorced, no children, a retired psych nurse who had worked his entire career at Havenwood.

Austin made sure to look non-threatening. At least as much as a man his height and build could. He wore a cable knit sweater over a button-down shirt, dark jeans, and hiking boots. Since the day was sunny and the temperature hovered above freezing, he'd left his heavy parka in the 4Runner so he looked somewhat smaller.

Then he smiled and rang the doorbell.

Wade was a short, stocky man with a fringe of white hair around a bald dome. He wore a faded Adirondack Flames hockey sweatshirt, sweatpants with the logo of the local community college, and a well-worn pair of suede and sheepskin slippers.

"Who are you?" Wade's rough voice suggested a lifelong pack-a-day habit.

"I'm working on an article about Havenwood—hundred and fiftieth anniversary and all," Austin said pleasantly. "I understand you worked there, and I'd like to ask you a few questions."

Wade looked him up and down. "You look like a cop."

"I'm not a cop." *Not anymore.*

"Whaddya want to know?"

"Havenwood did cutting edge work for its time," Austin replied, coming at this from a different angle than he'd used before. "I want to make sure to give credit to the doctors and their teams that made that possible. I know you worked with Jonah Neeson and Steve Ramsey, and I've heard good things, but I can't figure out which of the medical staff led your team."

Wade eyed him mistrustfully but hadn't kicked him out yet, which Austin took as a win.

"Where'd ya say this is gonna run?"

"*The Albany Times*," Austin replied, figuring he might need a cover story. "It would be a shame for the hospital's good work to be forgotten." *And if this blows the lid off an old kidnapping ring, they probably will run a story.*

Wade looked like he was considering the question. "I worked for a lot of the docs over the years. But they sent the hard cases to Doc Huffman. He handled the ones no one else could deal with."

"Those are the kinds of stories people want to hear," Austin said. "Were those cases violent? Delusional?"

"Sometimes both," Wade replied. "He got the strange ones, the kids who thought they were wolves or witches or talked to ghosts. He worked with them, and sometimes they got better."

Austin managed to keep from showing his reaction in his expression. "That sounds like you had your work cut out for you. Pretty crazy stuff, even for Havenwood."

"We didn't use that word." Wade's reaction was automatic, old habit. "Although that's what the families that sent those kids to us thought. Sometimes we could talk the patients out of believing they could do strange things. Other times, we couldn't."

"The ones who couldn't be helped, what happened to them?"

The wariness returned to Wade's features. "It was a big place. If they transferred off our unit, it was hard to keep track."

He's lying.

"You don't happen to remember a boy named Thomas McKean, do you? His name came up—"

"We're done."

"But—"

"I said we're done." Wade's eyes had gone hard and cold. "And here's a tip for your article. You've got a hundred years of Havenwood to talk about. Leave Huffman out of it."

He slammed the door.

Austin glanced over his shoulder when he walked back to the car and saw Wade peering from behind the curtains, making sure he left.

Must have hit a nerve. Good.

Austin had turned off the ringer on his phone while he talked to Wade. He left the angry man's driveway and drove to a nearby parking lot, then pulled out his phone to check for missed calls. He immediately clicked on a text from Jamie.

Jamie: *It's more fun to do research when you're here.*

Austin smiled, pleased that Jamie was missing him. He'd been aware of Jamie's absence all morning. And while he knew that meant his heart was heading in a dangerous direction, Austin had no intention of changing anything.

Austin: *Wish you were here. We could play "good cop, bad cop" like in the movies.*

He waited a few minutes, and when Jamie didn't reply, Austin figured he'd gotten busy with work. Just as he was about to pull out of the lot, a response came through.

Jamie: *Can we have fake badges with rock star names like on TV?*

Austin: *You know it doesn't actually work like that, right?*

Then again, he'd been posing as a reporter, so maybe Jamie wasn't too far off.

Jamie: *Don't destroy my illusions!* Jamie had added some emojis for emphasis.

Austin stopped for lunch and traded a few texts with

Jamie as he ate. Then he got back on the road and put the next address into his GPS, hoping he'd have more luck with this one. *Third time's the charm.*

The next name on Austin's list was Susan Lockwood, a Registered Nurse, retired, seventy-seven, one son. The house at the end of the long driveway was a modern log cabin in need of maintenance. An overgrown yard and a fallen downspout made him wonder if anyone still lived there.

A man in his fifties opened the door and eyed Austin with weary resignation. "If you're here about the taxes, or the mortgage or the bills...I'm working on it. You'll get your money as soon as I can figure out what she owes." He moved to close the door but hesitated at Austin's smile.

"I'm not a bill collector. I was looking for Susan Lockwood because she worked at Havenwood Hospital and I'm doing an article about the history of the place."

"She's not here," the man said. "Mom hasn't been well for a while," he added, with a general gesture toward the yard, the house, and everything around them. "I'm her son, Bob. We just moved her to a memory assistance unit last month."

"I'm sorry to hear that." Austin's sincerity must have come through in his voice. He wasn't Grandma Helen's caregiver—that task fell to his mother—but he'd seen first-hand the toll it took.

"What paper are you with?"

"It's for a retrospective on the hospital, for the paper in Albany. I heard about your mom from some of the people she worked with." *If I find out what happened to all the missing people, I don't doubt that Havenwood will make the headlines in Albany. Just not the way he might expect.*

To his surprise, Bob opened the door. "Come in. I can tell you what I remember if that's any help. Didn't work there myself, but Mom talked some about what she did over the years. Not names or anything confidential," he added quickly. "Just general stuff, but it might help."

"Thank you." Austin followed him into the house, where most of the floor and much of the furniture were covered with piles of books, magazines, and miscellaneous stuff.

"Sorry for the mess. I'm trying to get a handle on it. Mom made it sound like she had it together, but obviously she didn't," Bob said with a sigh. "I've been working down in Utica, and it's been about a year since I've been to the house. The last few times I came to visit, Mom wanted us to get a motel in Lake George or Lake Placid 'like a little vacation,' she said. Now I realize she didn't want me to see how bad it had gotten."

"I'm sorry."

Bob shrugged. "It is what it is. Happens to lots of other people every day. Guess it was just my turn." He paused and offered a chagrined half-smile. "I'm sorry—I should have offered you coffee. I just made a fresh pot—pretty much run on the stuff to keep moving."

Austin declined, but Bob refreshed his own mug and came back to shove enough piles out of the way for them both to sit. "Now, tell me what kind of information you're looking for."

Austin repeated the version of his cover story that had worked a little better with Wade. When he finished, Bob nodded. "Okay. Maybe I can help a little. It won't be first-hand, but Mom really isn't up for an interview, even if she might recall back then better than what happened yesterday."

He drew a breath and let it out again. "Havenwood—like the other places of its kind—was a product of the times. Even the professionals didn't know much about mental illness; they had prejudices that called all kinds of things 'sick' which weren't, and the laws made it easy to offload an inconvenient person to become a ward of the state."

Austin nodded, familiar with enough history to know Bob was right.

"The ones who had it the worst—then and now—were the kids who didn't have a family or who had shitty parents. They got packed off to jail or a psych ward for just about any excuse so they'd be someone else's problem." He paused to sip his coffee. "Havenwood had its share of those folks—as well as people with genuine psychiatric issues."

He met Austin's gaze. "My mother was a psychiatric nurse. She knew medicine and psychology, and she had a big heart. Sometimes she'd come home from a shift, and I'd find her in the kitchen crying because there was only so much she could do."

"She sounds like a pretty special lady."

"She's the best," Bob replied, with a grateful smile directed at Austin for the comment. "My dad died when I was in high school, so it was just Mom and me. We probably talked about a lot more adult topics than my friends did with their parents because there wasn't anyone else around. I remember a couple of things clearly."

He sipped his coffee again, and Austin thought the other man looked nervous, maybe worried about the reaction to what he was about to say. "She didn't like the big-shot doctor. Sometimes she had to work with him, but she didn't trust him. Never said what she thought he was doing, of course. Now, with all the stuff that's in the news, it makes me wonder."

Austin's heart sank, although he wasn't surprised. Institutions like Havenwood didn't have a good track record on protecting their vulnerable patients from predators.

"A skeevy doc isn't big news. But more than once, she talked about how she thought some of the kids had a 'shine' to them. That's the word she used—'shine.' Like in that Stephen King movie with Jack Nicholson? She meant a little *something extra.*"

Bob's expression challenged Austin to discount his story. When Austin didn't say anything, Bob went on. "There was one boy who they said was psychotic because he talked to invisible people. Then she overheard him one night and recognized the name of his 'friend.' Got him to describe his new buddy. Everything he said checked out—but the friend was another boy who had died on that wing a couple of years before." Bob added with a pointed look at Austin.

"That wasn't the only time. There were others who knew stuff before it happened or knew what people were thinking. Spooky things like that. Of course, no one believed them—but she did."

"Did any of those younger patients ever go missing?"

Bob sighed. "I don't know. There were some patients who 'ran off' now and again, but I couldn't tell you if it included any of those particular people."

Austin had heard that for many people, "extra" abilities showed up around puberty. Not always—some were much earlier or later. But Austin's own "hunches" had started around that time. Grandma Helen had told him that it ran in the family and not to worry. She seemed more comfortable with the topic than Austin's mother, and he'd always wondered if the family "gift" had skipped a generation.

But I don't think Grandma Helen has the ability herself. Did Thomas? And if he did, was that why he was sent away?

"Is there anything else your mother might have said that might be good for my article?" Austin probed.

Bob thought for a moment. "Mom kept journals. I

haven't had a chance to look at them, but let me page through and see if there's anything that might be useful. I suspect it'll be mostly about family stuff, but if you can leave me a card, I'll call you if I find something." He gave Austin a wan smile. "It'll give me a purpose to look through them instead of feeling sad."

Austin handed him his business card and thanked Bob as they walked to the door.

"I should be thanking you," Bob replied. "It gets too quiet here by myself, and I've been gone long enough I don't know anyone in town anymore. So thanks for the diversion."

When Austin pulled out of the driveway, he had only been on the road for a few minutes before he looked in his mirror and saw a police cruiser following him. He checked his speed and knew he was within the limit. The 4Runner had just been in for inspection, so the tags were current, and all his lights worked.

He expected the cruiser to pass when they came to a stretch with a dotted center line. It didn't, hanging behind him steadily enough to be ominous.

When its lights turned on without warning, Austin thought it might swing around him to respond to a call. Instead, it closed the distance between them, tailgating him until he pulled off onto the wide shoulder.

Dark suspicions rose in Austin's mind. The first two men he had interviewed certainly hadn't warmed to his line of questioning, and they'd had enough time to call a buddy on the local force and ask for a favor. He didn't like where that line of thinking led him.

Austin waited with his hands on the wheel and lowered his window when the cop sauntered up to the car. Between his hat and sunglasses, Austin couldn't get a good look at the man's face, and his concern deepened when he realized the cop's name tag was conspicuously missing.

"What seems to be the matter, officer?" Austin asked, polite but confident. He knew his rights, and he also knew that by speaking first, he got the upper hand, however briefly.

"Someone saw a strange car pulling into driveways where it didn't belong and reported it—like good neighbors do," the cop replied. "Car just like yours."

"Just visiting some folks," Austin replied. "Sorry to have alarmed the neighborhood watch."

"Folks hereabouts like their privacy," the cop told him, hooking his thumbs in his belt. "Don't like strangers showing up uninvited. You might want to try calling first. Nearly everyone in these parts hunts. You wouldn't want to end up with an ass full of buckshot—or worse."

Austin knew a threat when he heard one. "I'll keep that in mind."

He kept his posture relaxed but alert and held his gaze steady at those mirrored sunglasses, not escalating but not backing down either. They both knew the cop didn't have anything on him, but plenty of innocent people had ended up dead from traffic stops. All the cop needed to do afterward would be to draw attention to Austin's gun and claim that he feared for his life. Small town like this, there wouldn't even be an inquest.

"See that you do," the cop replied, slapping the roof of the SUV hard for emphasis.

Austin didn't move until the cop was back in his cruiser and finally pulled away. He waited until the car was out of sight, then pulled out, did a U-turn, and headed back the way he came, in the opposite direction of where the cruiser had gone.

He drove back to town, fighting to regain a decent mood. Austin thought about stopping by the Historical Association and then remembered that Jamie had mentioned an evening work event. Still, there was always time for a quick text, and even if Jamie didn't see it until later, he'd know Austin was thinking about him.

Austin: *Missed you today. Looking forward to seeing you tomorrow.*

To his surprise, the answer came back in seconds.

Jamie: *Missed you too. I'd much rather be spending the evening with you. See you in the morning.*

He thought about mentioning the incident with the cop but didn't want to commit that to a text message. Austin had already warned Jamie that digging up old scandals might be dangerous. Jamie hadn't been with him today to draw the cop's attention, and other than talking with the old men at the diner, all of his sleuthing had occurred in the privacy of the Historical Association. Still, Austin fretted, remembering his visions and the images of Jamie in danger.

Austin: *Be careful.*

Jamie: *You too.*

The text banter gave Austin a warm feeling, and he could admit to himself that he had a crush on Jamie.

Could this become something more? Albany isn't that far away. We could visit on weekends, stay in touch through the week...it's been way too long since anyone got to me like he does. I was starting to think I'd never find "the one." I know it's early but...could Jamie be it for me?

The idea thrilled and scared him. Austin liked the idea of settling down with someone, but so far none of his relationships had turned into the "forever" kind of thing. They hadn't always blown up spectacularly or led to days bingeing ice cream or alcohol in an angsty stupor. Most of the time, the pairings had just fizzled out, without enough substance to keep them strong once the newness of the sexual attraction finally waned.

He couldn't imagine his interest in Jamie decreasing, although they'd barely begun to explore one another. But aside from how crazy hot he thought Jamie was, Austin enjoyed their conversations. And while Jamie's interest in superheroes didn't quite match Austin's, and Austin had never read a romance novel, they both seemed willing to try new things to meet each other halfway.

Maybe.... Austin felt a spark of hope. He intended to fan that flame and see what came from it.

He parked in front of his room at the motel and decided to walk into town to get coffee and dinner. The stroll to the Sunrise Café felt good after spending much of the day in the car, and he loved the tang of balsam in the air despite the chill.

The Café was busy, so Austin took a seat at the counter and asked for a large coffee-to-go. After he studied the menu, he ordered the special—a hamburger topped with Swiss cheese, mushrooms, and onions—as well as a side of what Canadians called "poutine" and Americans referred to as "garbage fries"—French fries and cheese curds covered in gravy. While he waited, he sipped his coffee and glanced around the restaurant, observing the other diners.

Couples and families took up most of the tables, with a few solo diners here and there. Near the back, a trio of older men had a loud conversation going—lively enough that he wondered if it might end in punches thrown. Since no one else paid any attention, Austin figured this was normal.

In between their arguments, the men joked with two local cops at the next table, and even without hearing what was said, Austin could tell the men had a long history.

"Here's your order," the server behind the counter said, bringing his burger and fries in a paper bag. "Want me to top off your coffee before you head out?"

Austin let her refill the cup as he paid the tab and left a generous tip. When she returned with his change, he realized that one of the men was glaring daggers in his direction. Austin wondered if they knew either of the grumpy men he had tried to interview earlier in the day.

That's my cue to get out of here.

Austin grabbed his bag and cup and headed for the door. He knew someone was behind him as he stepped out into the parking lot, but he didn't expect to feel a hand fall heavily on his shoulder.

"I'd like a word with you."

Austin figured the speaker was one of the local cops just from the voice. He turned slowly. A glance at the uniform told him it was the sheriff this time. "Can I help you, Sheriff?"

Now that he got a good look at the man, Austin knew he'd seen his kind before, back in Albany. *There's no one quite as self-important as a small-town lawman.* The guy was probably in his early forties, and from the way he held himself, Austin bet he'd been the high school quarterback and maybe the homecoming king. Now that he had a badge, a uniform, and a gun, he probably figured he'd reached the pinnacle of manhood.

"I hear you've been harassing senior citizens. We don't look kindly on that sort of thing."

Austin had been a cop, and he knew his rights. Even more importantly, his fries were getting soggy. "Am I under arrest for something?" he asked, giving the sheriff a no-nonsense look.

"No, but—"

"Am I free to go?" Austin knew how to play the game. And if the cop insisted on being an asshole, Austin had a few lawyer friends back in Albany who could make short work of any bogus charges.

"Yeah, but watch your step. You don't want to make trouble here."

Austin bit back a dozen responses that came to mind and walked away. He half expected the sheriff to follow him but realized after a few blocks that he hadn't. *This time.*

He grumbled a string of curses and felt slightly better for it. By the time he reached the hotel, he had finished his coffee. Austin dumped the empty cup in a garbage bin and went into the office to get a soda from the vending machine.

Greg was behind the desk. "You doin' okay?" he asked, with an expression that warned Austin the question was more than polite chatter.

"Yeah. At least I think so. Why?" Austin tried to keep his tone neutral as he fed quarters into the machine and hoped his fries wouldn't be a cold mushy mess by the time he made it to his room.

"Just wondering. Heard you've been asking questions." Greg shrugged in reply to Austin's raised eyebrow. "Small town. Word gets around."

"Is that a problem?"

Greg shook his head. "Not for me. And I'm sure you've got your reasons. But a word to the wise—tread lightly. There are people in this town you don't want to cross."

Greg didn't sound threatening—more like a true warning from someone who knew the area. Austin did his best to keep from bristling, knowing he needed all the allies he could find. "Thanks. I'll keep that in mind."

He was ready to leave and then turned. "That genealogy research? Turns out my great-uncle was reported missing.

No one knows why or what happened to him. I'm going to do my best to find out."

"This have anything to do with Havenwood Hospital?"

Austin considered denying it, then nodded. "Yeah. You know anything about the hospital?"

Greg shook his head. "Not personally. But I do know folks around here are real protective of their history—even if it doesn't deserve being protected." He offered a conspiratorial smile. "Your dinner smells good. Better get it eaten before it goes cold."

The food was lukewarm when he unwrapped it, so he put it in the microwave. It was still delicious, and Austin was hungry. His phone buzzed, and he saw another text from Jamie.

Jamie: *You're so much more fun than this dreary fundraiser. Maybe I'll dream something exciting. I'll be thinking of you.*

Austin: *Been thinking of you all day. I imagine I'll have exciting dreams as well. See you bright and early.*

Austin downed the soda and then poured himself a drink from the bottle of whiskey he'd brought with him, enjoying the burn as the liquor unsnarled the tension that had built up over the day. He'd made progress—he was sure of that, even if he wasn't entirely certain toward what.

This is bigger than just Thomas. Did he have a bit of "shine"? Was he sent away because someone was afraid of him—or thought he had the devil? And if he did have abilities, was that how he escaped? Or was he taken or killed because of his shine?

Someone knows. Now all I have to do is get them to tell me.

Austin got ready for bed, loosened up by the whiskey and tired from the efforts of the day. Back in Albany, his grandmother's house held the heat enough that he could sleep in a T-shirt and boxer briefs. The motel room was drafty, and Austin opted for a loose pair of flannel sleep pants.

Tired as he was, his cock filled quickly to thoughts of Jamie. Austin slicked his palm with lube, and the drawstring of his pants easily accommodated sliding a hand inside to stroke his length while he imagined how he'd like one of their nights to go.

I haven't seen him naked yet. I bet he's beautiful. Austin's pictured seeing the chest his hands had mapped beneath Jamie's shirt. Toned muscle, tight abs, slim hips. Sparse hair on his chest and more on his thighs. He'd glimpsed a nest of dark curls when he'd given Jamie the hand job, just like he'd caught a look at his cock. And not a peek yet at that perfect ass.

In his imagination, he peeled away Jamie's shirt, then opened his belt and unzipped the fly, easing jeans and boxer-briefs down his thighs, then to his ankles and gone completely. He appreciated a clear view of Jamie's cock and balls before going down on him with gusto. He thought of discovering the taste of Jamie's pre-come, the feel of his lover's stiff dick in his mouth, and swallowing him down as he climaxed, with Austin's fingers digging into Jamie's fine ass.

Austin came, biting his lip to stay quiet, as his release spurted over his fist. He lay still, panting and sweaty, wishing he could hold Jamie in his arms as they fell asleep, both of them sated and happy.

I'm already in over my head. He's special...am I crazy to hope we can make something more of this thing between us than just a fling? And can I keep him safe long enough for us to find out?

Austin knew he wouldn't find that answer tonight. He cleaned up in the bathroom and changed his T-shirt, then slipped back beneath the covers, sure that despite the questions in his mind, he would sleep well tonight.

And he did—until the vision struck.

Shots fired. Austin heard himself shouting. He saw Jamie bound and bloodied on the floor, still fighting his captors. Austin dodged another bullet that lodged in the plaster wall beside him and realized he'd end up dead if he didn't keep his attention on his attacker.

Austin heard a man scream and then the thump of a body tumbling down steps.

"Jamie!" he shouted. "Jamie!"

Austin sat bolt upright in bed. His heart thudded, and cold sweat made his T-shirt cling to his back.

A glance at the alarm clock beside his bed told him it was three in the morning. Far too late to call Jamie and reassure himself the other man was safe.

We were together in the vision, so it can't happen to him without me being there.

That offered scant comfort. Austin hadn't seen the faces of their attackers, and the dark scene gave him no idea of where they might have been.

Maybe if I stick close to him, I'll be nearby to protect him, and I won't have to explain about my dreams. At least, not until we've had time to figure out this attraction between us and learn to trust each other.

If I tell him I see visions, he might freak out and tell me to get lost. Then I can't protect him at all. So I'll just warn him again that some of the people involved might still be around and not want me digging into the past, and then I'll do my best to make sure he doesn't get hurt.

Austin's heart rate slowed, finally. He shivered and told himself it was because the cool air hit his damp shirt, but the fear from his vision was bone deep.

It's my fault he's in danger. Whatever happened here is a lot bigger than just my missing great-uncle. Someone out there knows the truth—and wants to keep it hidden. So I'll stay close enough to keep Jamie safe and see if we can get justice for Thomas and the others.

Without getting either of us killed.

6

JAMIE

Despite only spending a couple of evenings with Austin, the investigator had gotten under Jamie's skin. Today seemed to go on forever, and the evening fundraiser was painfully boring. Jamie forced a smile and mingled with the patrons, trying to keep his mind on his work when his thoughts were far more focused on the mystery he and Austin had begun to untangle.

He locked up the Historical Association once the reception finished and headed back to his apartment. Jamie usually had at least one, maybe two late nights each week, although tonight's reception went later than most, wrapping up at ten. By the time he'd done basic clean up, it was closer to eleven before he made his final pass to check everything.

The ghosts were more noisy than usual once all the human guests had gone. Jamie heard footsteps on the stairs and tromping across the second floor. The chandelier pendants on the fancy lamp jangled hard enough he feared something would shatter. A door slammed. Jamie had never been so glad to set the alarm and lock the door.

Saranac Lake was quiet at this hour. The last movie

ended at eleven, and a few restaurants and bars were still open, but most businesses closed much earlier. In the summer, the sidewalks might still be filled with tourists taking a stroll or the people just leaving concerts in the park. But this was not peak season, and the people who remained were mostly year-round residents. They were home in front of the TV by now or getting ready for bed. Definitely not out for a walk.

Jamie realized he should have driven, even though the distance was normally an easy walk. He hunched his shoulders against the wind, jammed his hands into the pockets of his coat, and picked up his pace. He didn't see anyone else outside, but in the cold light of the street lamps, Jamie felt exposed and vulnerable.

I'd feel safer if Austin were here.

Austin moved with a confidence that warned others not to mess with him. Jamie could win a battle of words, but short of throwing a book at an attacker, he doubted he'd be much good in a fight. He hoped he never had to find out.

Jamie glanced nervously over his shoulder. He couldn't shake the feeling that someone was following him. Nothing unusual had occurred at the reception, and his boss had been too busy schmoozing donors to say more than a few words to him, most of them about putting out more *hors d'oeuvres* or refreshing the wine bar.

This wasn't the first time he'd gone home late after an event, and it usually didn't bother him since Saranac Lake had such a low crime rate. Jamie had never felt unsafe before, locking up at night by himself. Although tonight, the ghosts had been more riled up than usual, which also put him on edge.

He thought about calling Austin, and he knew the other man would answer. But he hesitated, unwilling to look like he couldn't handle himself. This thing between them was still too new, too undefined. He wanted to trust Austin, but past relationships warned him to be careful. Jamie hoped that they'd get to the point where he wasn't afraid to be himself—his whole self, fears and ghosts included. But they weren't there yet, and he didn't know if that future was in the cards, although he hoped so.

Ghosts. How do I tell him I see ghosts?

In the past, disclosing that ability had never gone well. One boyfriend laughed out loud and was sure Jamie was pranking him. Another had spent a little too much time with role-playing games and wouldn't believe Jamie didn't have full conversations with spirits and couldn't summon the dead.

Jamie didn't want to see disappointment or disbelief in Austin's eyes. He really hoped they could make more of their attraction than a short fling, but if not, then he didn't want to spoil the time they had.

If this turns into something serious, there'll be time to explain. There's no hurry.

Jamie reached his apartment and froze. The light by the door he always left on was dark, its glass lantern smashed. Trash had been dumped all over the porch—but only on his side of the duplex. No one left food scrap garbage out where raccoons or bears could get into it, but he had felt safe putting clean paper trash in a secure steel can tucked into the corner of the railing. It took a hard yank to get the lid off, so there was no way the mess could be blamed on the wind.

Then Jamie noticed that the screen door had been slit from top to bottom. Not torn by animal claws. Cut cleanly, like by a knife.

Anger carried him forward, afraid that whoever had vandalized his place had also broken into his apartment. For a moment, he considered calling the cops, but his gut warned against it. Jamie wanted to call Austin, but he didn't want to blow the situation out of proportion. After all, no actual damage had been done other than to the screen and outside light. He didn't have a security camera, and the cops were likely to dismiss the whole thing as a prank by local teens. Still, Jamie pulled out his phone and took pictures, going as quickly as he could so he didn't have to remain outside longer than necessary.

To his relief, the door was still locked, but just in case, he grabbed the garbage can lid and a broom from the porch, holding them like a shield and sword as he entered the duplex.

Jamie locked the door behind him and flicked on the light, tense and ready for a fight. He made his way warily through the small house, sweeping back the shower curtain with the broom handle, jerking closet doors open, sure he might have a heart attack if he actually did find an intruder.

Every light blazed by the time he was done, and Jamie thought he might sleep with them on tonight for good measure.

He'd clean up the porch in the morning. Maybe by daylight, he'd be able to tell that it had been a wild animal, or perhaps local homophobic jerks. Perhaps his neighbor had seen or heard something—Jamie intended to ask first thing tomorrow. They didn't know each other well, but they had traded greetings. Jamie vaguely remembered that the man had said he worked nights, although he didn't mention his hours.

The adrenaline of the fright waned, and the long day caught up with Jamie in a rush, leaving him spent. Much as he knew it would be comforting to hear Austin's voice, he wasn't up to giving a recap right now and decided that he would tell Austin about the incident tomorrow.

Jamie put the garbage can lid by the door along with the broom and hung up his coat. Then he changed into sweats and drank a cup of hot chocolate, noticing how his hands were shaking. He double-checked that all of the windows and the back door were locked, turned on the light by the garage, and shoved a chair under the doorknob for good measure. After that, Jamie decided he'd earned a little time off.

Since he'd been working all evening and hadn't been able to avail himself of the wine bar, he splashed a generous dollop of Bailey's and a double-shot of whipped cream vodka into his hot chocolate, a reward for surviving both the reception and the vandalism to his apartment.

Maybe I'm not cut out for the director's role, he thought, grabbing a bag of chips and heading for the couch. *I loathe evenings like tonight.*

Then again, if I was somewhere I planned to stay for a while, where I could make a real difference and develop plans for the future, maybe chatting up donors wouldn't be torture. I know how I get when I'm passionate about something. How many times have I managed to convince all my friends to try my new favorite show, song, book, game? I'm pretty good at that—if it's something I believe in.

I knew when I took the job that it would be temporary. Looks good on the resume, great experience. I wish I had a clue about what comes next.

He switched on the TV and parked on reruns of Viking Week on The History Channel. Jamie sipped his Bailey's hot chocolate and flicked open the text messages on his phone, smiling as he read down through the conversation he'd managed with Austin.

I really like him. Probably more than I should. He's got a hot body and a nice smile. He's a good kisser. Now that I've stroked him off, I want to get a much better look at that package—I've got all kinds of ideas for how to get better acquainted. I bet he's got a great ass. We need to get naked.

A dog's frantic barking interrupted Jamie's thoughts. Concerned, he set his drink aside and went to the window as his heart began to pound again. He recognized the high-pitched bark of his neighbor's Schnauzer, Bismarck, and wondered what set him off. Just as Jamie was about to dismiss the barking as a false alarm, he thought he spotted a shadow moving along the bushes between the duplex and the next house. He couldn't make out the details, but the shape looked more like a hunched man than any kind of animal.

Spooked, Jamie closed the drapes and double-checked the lock on the door, sliding a kitchen chair under the door-knob of the front door as well. He reclaimed his still-warm cup and huddled into the corner of the couch.

What the fuck? Did the person who trashed my porch come back for round two? Most of the gay-bashing bullies I've met don't work that hard, and a burglar wouldn't have made that kind of mess. Anyone who thinks I've got something here worth stealing is badly mistaken.

Unless...could it have something to do with Austin's project? He was afraid digging up old secrets wouldn't be popular and warned me to be careful earlier tonight. Is someone trying to scare me off the case?

If so, they were going to be sorely disappointed. Jamie always figured that if he had a superpower, it was stubborn-ness. That had gotten him through college and grad school when he had to work two jobs to pay tuition. It had given him the courage to stand up to patronizing professors and bosses who tried to cheat him out of hours.

If some asshole thinks he's going to run me off from helping Austin figure out what happened to his great-uncle and all the others, they've got another think coming. The people who went missing and their families deserve justice. And I'm not going to let Austin do it by himself.

Jamie finished his drink and felt the alcohol go straight to his head after the long day. He switched off the TV, checked all the doors and windows one more time, peeked outside to assure himself no one was skulking around, and got ready for bed.

He slipped under the sheets, comfortable beneath the warm blankets, boneless from exhaustion and his drink. Jamie fell asleep imagining that he was sleeping next to Austin, safe and protected.

———

THE NEXT MORNING, Jamie took the time to jerk off in the shower, remembering the fantasies about Austin that had lulled him to sleep the night before. Together with a hot cup of coffee and a muffin, that made for a good start to the day —at least until he remembered the mess from the night before.

With a sigh, Jamie grabbed his phone and pulled on his coat and boots. He walked onto the porch and put his hands on his hips, surveying the damage, then took another set of photos in daylight, along with a closeup of the damaged screen and broken light. Picking up the trash was easy, but to avoid a repeat of last night, he carried the can to the garage. He figured it might be easier to just pay to replace the glass shade on the outside light and the cut screen himself rather than explain what happened.

It could have been a lot worse. But who did it—and what did they want?

Jamie decided to drive since he had another event that evening. He could park right next to the Historical Association's back door, meaning he only had to cover a few feet to be safe. Despite his short drive, Jamie cranked up the radio and focused on looking forward to seeing Austin. He wondered how yesterday had gone for him.

I'm crushing on him like a teenager. And it feels good.

Austin brought coffee and fresh donuts to the association, just as Jamie had hoped. When they took the goodies into the break room, Jamie stretched up for a kiss. "Thank you. I'm glad you're here—and not just for the crullers."

Austin kissed him back with enough heat that Jamie hoped no customers walked in soon because he'd never hide the bulge in his dress pants. "Keep that up, and I'll thank you for donuts more often," Jamie joked.

Austin grabbed a chocolate iced glazed donut and took a big bite. Then he kissed Jamie again, and Jamie could taste chocolate and sugar on his lips.

"Actually, I really needed this," Austin confessed. "Someone keyed my car overnight."

Jamie's eyes widened. "Did you call the police?"

Austin stuck his head out of the doorway to check that they were still alone. He turned back to Jamie. "I think it might have *been* the police."

Jamie's eyebrows rose. "Oh?"

Austin filled him in about the incident with the cop on the way back from his interviews and the sheriff at Sunrise Café, keeping his voice low so it didn't carry. "Pretty sure at least one of the two men I tried to interview must have ratted me out. By the time I got back to my room, the gossip had made it around town all the way to Greg at the motel's front desk."

Jamie looked at him, alarmed. "I knew this was a small town. I didn't realize it was *that* small." He hesitated for a moment, then gathered his nerve. "I felt like I was being followed last night, on my way home. When I got there, my porch was trashed, and someone cut the screen and broke the light. Then later on, the neighbor's dog barked his fool head off, and I thought I saw something in the shadows."

"I don't like the sound of that," Austin said, covering Jamie's hand with his. "Did your neighbor see anything?"

Jamie shook his head. "I called first thing this morning. He said he called off work with a migraine and took some heavy-duty pain pills. According to him, a bomb could have gone off, and he wouldn't have noticed."

"Shit," Austin said. They finished their coffee while Austin told Jamie about the rest of his interviews, including the theory that Susan's son, Bob, had shared.

"So you think that your great-uncle might have been, what—a psychic or something?" Jamie asked, realizing that he was on the verge of holding his breath. *If Austin believes in psychics...maybe seeing ghosts isn't too crazy.*

"I don't know," Austin confessed. "I called Grandma Helen, and she had never heard anyone say that about Thomas." Austin's expression made Jamie wonder if there was part of that conversation he wasn't sharing.

"Do you think the doctor was some sort of religious fanatic?" Jamie asked, horrified. "Did he *get rid* of patients he thought were evil?"

Austin shrugged. "I don't know. I'm sure he wasn't in it alone. There's something we're missing or something that's right in front of us that we aren't seeing clearly."

Jamie put a hand on his arm. "We'll figure it out. Together."

Austin smiled and let his fingers trace down Jamie's cheek. "Thank you. I just don't want to cause trouble for you. I feel like what happened last night is my fault."

Jamie laid a finger over Austin's lips. "Hush. We had this conversation already. And we don't know for certain that what happened to me had anything to do with your project, although it pays to be careful. The bottom line is that people went missing, and their families deserve answers. I've got your back."

They set their cups aside and headed into the main room. The door chime would have let them know if anyone had entered, so Jamie knew they still had the place to themselves. He headed to the work table they had shared before.

"I've been combing through the donated memory boxes and gathering everything that mentions Havenwood. I figured we could work our way through it and see what we find," Jamie said.

They made themselves comfortable and dug in. It didn't take long for the table to be covered with newspaper articles, old photographs, diaries, and odd papers. Tackling the pile didn't seem quite so daunting with both of them working. After a few hours, with Jamie taking the occasional break to work with customers, Austin sat back in his chair and stretched.

"I've got pages of notes on everything we found about Havenwood, but I'm still not sure what it means," he admitted.

"We've got the names of the senior medical staff and Dr. Huffman's core team," Jamie pointed out. "We know that Vincent Huffman left Havenwood suddenly in 1980, and that's when the disappearances ended."

"The rest of the senior staff quit shortly afterward, and the department was reorganized." Havenwood had struggled on for another decade, only to close in the early 1990s after the aging facility was deemed too expensive to bring up to code.

"He headed the section for adolescent and young adult patients," Jamie replied. "So your theory about teenagers being committed because they were just coming into their abilities and didn't know how to handle them—or hide them—might be true."

Austin nodded. "A kid has to deal with hormones and then starts getting visions or knowing things he has no way to know, or seeing ghosts." He didn't seem to notice Jamie's flinch at that last comment. "He freaks out—or accidentally hurts someone. Or he's got parents who would have fit in at the Salem Witch Trials, who think anything paranormal comes from the devil."

Unfortunately, Jamie had met people like that—one of the reasons he learned to be careful who he told about his "ability."

"Do you think Huffman killed the patients?" That made Jamie's heart hurt.

Austin shrugged. "I don't know. *Something* happened. I want to think they got away, but I can't imagine that's the answer for all of them."

"How about setting that question aside for a minute," Jamie said. "Take a look at these—they're the floor plans I told you about."

Austin perked up when Jamie brought out the folio. "That's impressive. Havenwood is a big place."

Jamie nodded, grinning. "And there are different versions of the plans over the years, so we can see how it changed. Maybe that'll give us ideas of how the patients might have gotten away—or been taken out without anyone noticing."

They leaned over the floor plans and into each other's space, bumping shoulders, easy and comfortable. Austin's eyes were alight with excitement, and Jamie loved seeing him like this. Even if the topic was sobering, Austin's delight at finding something tangible they could work with warmed Jamie's heart.

"Look," Austin said, touching Jamie lightly on the arm to get his attention. "There were service corridors and stairways, dumbwaiters, and an elevator in the newer wing for laundry and supplies."

Jamie nodded, understanding where Austin was going with his comment. "And in the basement, one of those tunnels went to the morgue—probably so other patients wouldn't be upset seeing a body taken out."

"It wouldn't have been hard to move a person out to the laundry trucks or a hearse," Austin said quietly. "Especially if they were drugged and bound."

"Jesus," Jamie murmured at the image Austin's words brought to mind. "The laundry trucks might have been a way to escape as well." He wasn't ready to believe the worst.

"I need to go have a look at the hospital," Austin said. "There's still something we're missing."

"*We* need to go," Jamie repeated, meeting Austin's gaze. "Together."

Austin looked like he intended to protest, but Jamie set his jaw in the expression his mother had always called his "mule look." "Not up for debate," Jamie added. "Safer with two."

"You could get fired if we get caught."

"Temporary job, remember? This is more important."

Austin leaned forward and brushed his lips lightly against Jamie's temple. "Thank you."

"When do you want to go?" Jamie asked.

"I'd rather go in daylight, although we'll need to find a place to park the car so it won't be obvious," Austin mused.

"Tomorrow's Sunday. We're closed all day."

"If we go early, we can be in and out before too many people are up and around," Austin said. "Even the cops like to take it easy on Sunday mornings."

"Works for me."

Austin grinned. "Good. That's settled. How about dinner tonight?"

Jamie sighed. "It's Community Night—we have an author coming from seven to nine to talk about his new book about the history of ice fishing in the Adirondacks. And then I'll have to clean up."

Austin gave him a crafty look. "You still have to eat. What if I make a food run and bring something back for both of us? We can eat in the break room. And if you want, you could spend the night with me at the motel so you'd be safer, and we could, um, get an early start in the morning."

The heat in Austin's gaze coupled with the slightly nervous tone in his voice suggested that he imagined more possibilities than rising early. Jamie hoped his smile made it clear that he was open to ideas.

"Sure, but I probably won't get there until close to eleven by the time I go home and grab an overnight bag."

"I'm willing if you are."

Jamie couldn't resist a smirk. "Oh, I'm very willing." He loved the flush that crept over Austin's face and down his neck.

Unfortunately, the chime on the front door sounded just then, and they moved apart just enough not to look like they were about to kiss. With a glance that promised he'd be back as soon as possible, Jamie went to deal with the customer.

"Mr. Quincey. Nice to see you again." Jamie recognized the old man from the diner, the one with the grumpy friends.

"And you as well," Quincey said. He glanced around, and his gaze lingered for a few seconds on Austin at the back table before returning to Jamie. "I came to drop off cookies for the event tonight. It was my turn to do refreshments, and I also checked the bulletin board at Sunrise Café and a couple of other places to make sure the notices were up." He held out two grocery bags with boxes of cookies, and Jamie took the contributions gracefully.

"I'll be back at quarter 'til seven to make a fresh pot of coffee and set up the cups and fixings," Quincey said. "I'm looking forward to hearing the speaker tonight. And it gives me a reason to go out other than eating," he added with a conspiratorial wink.

Jamie thanked him again and walked with him to the door, chatting about the weather and the price of gas. When he had seen the man off with a wave, he headed back to Austin.

"That's one of the old guys at Sunrise Café," Austin said. "I think his buddy is the one who sicced the cop on me."

Jamie sighed. "Ed. I know who you mean. Quincey is a sweetheart, but Ed's a jerk. If it's any consolation, he just about ripped me a new one for asking Quincey questions about the hospital."

"You think he knows something?"

Jamie shrugged. "Maybe. Or he's just a curmudgeon. Seems like a real 'get off my lawn' type."

Jamie sat at the table, and for the next few hours, they

worked through the items he'd flagged from the local history boxes. Austin took pictures of any photos of the hospital and noted the names of people who had worked at Havenwood when something related turned up. Jamie kept his own set of notes, which they agreed to pool at the end. He also made sure to photograph all of the hospital floor plans, which Jamie figured would come in handy when they went to have a look around.

Finally, Austin sat back and twisted his neck left and right to ease stiff muscles.

"Anything?" Jamie asked.

"A couple of people who worked there made comments about the daily routine, which might or might not be useful," Austin replied. "The property used to include a farm and animal barns. They thought that getting the patients out into the fresh air to do work if they were able was good exercise—and it helped the hospital be more self-sufficient for food. But there was no fence around the property, no razor-wire or guard turrets. Someone clever could have probably escaped."

"But probably not as many escapes as there were disappearances."

Austin grimaced. "Not unless their security was completely incompetent. So while it's possible some got out on their own, that doesn't account for everyone."

The alarm on his phone went off, and Austin glanced at the time. "That's my cue to go bring back dinner, so we have time to eat before your event. Do you need me to help you set up?"

Jamie appreciated the offer, but he shook his head. "Thanks, but it's not a big deal. We'll probably have five people, and I'll put out ten folding chairs, just in case. One or two will come because they're actually interested, and the others show up for the cookies."

"I can't blame them."

"The hard part is getting them to leave politely. It becomes a bit of a social hour, and I have to herd them toward the door, so I can get everything put away and shut down," Jamie added. "But guys like Quincey don't have a lot of other things to do, and it gets them out for something other than their weekly card game or bowling match."

Jamie hadn't minded the events before since he had nowhere better to be. But now that he was planning to spend the night with Austin, that changed things. *Maybe I'll hurry them a bit more than usual tonight.*

Austin returned quickly with their food, the spaghetti and meatballs blue plate special from the diner. They ate in the break room and kept the conversation light. After offering again to help with the chairs, Austin headed out to give Jamie time to prepare for the event. Jamie had Austin's phone number and knew which room he was in at the motel. Looking forward to afterward was going to make the night's program seem to take forever, but Jamie resolved to grin and bear it.

This might be a temporary job, but it's totally worth it if things work out with Austin.

7

AUSTIN

He'd already had supper, and Jamie was busy for the rest of the evening, which left Austin at loose ends. He stopped at a convenience store for snacks, soda, and beer so he could offer it if Jamie was hungry later. Feeling nervous and hopeful, Austin also picked up condoms and lube...just in case. A quick stop at the liquor store got him a new bottle of whiskey and some wine to go with the beer in his room. *That should cover a hot date.*

The strong attraction he felt for Jamie—in such a short period of time—surprised him. Scared him a little, if he was honest with himself. Austin realized, in hindsight, that he had allowed his personal life to drift on autopilot even as he stumbled through the plans he'd made for his career. Which hadn't quite gone the way he'd expected, either.

Getting pushed out of the Albany Police Department had done a number on his self-confidence. Until then, he thought he had everything under control. He had planned to make detective, then captain, retiring with commendations and a nice pension.

The accusations and mistrust over the advantages his secret abilities provided broke something in him. He understood that now, although it had taken a while to figure it out. He could no more stop being psychic than he could stop being gay—and he wouldn't want to. No one's approval was worth cutting out intrinsic parts of himself.

He'd been angry and gun shy about rejection after that, which only highlighted the problems in his relationships. Austin figured that he'd either subconsciously picked partners that weren't going to work out to validate his brokenness or pushed them away to avoid another betrayal. Eventually, he just stopped trying, telling himself "all the good ones are taken," although that didn't stop the loneliness.

Less than a week with Jamie had cracked Austin's heart wide open, with a terrifying rush of excitement and a level of desire Austin had never felt before.

Maybe I wasn't broken. Maybe I just hadn't found the right person.

Austin shook himself out of his thoughts as he unpacked his purchases in the hotel room. He still had several hours before Jamie's event ended, which gave him time to work on the case. Austin made a cup of coffee, sat at the table, and pulled out the notebook he'd used at the archive, along with the photos of Jamie's notes he'd taken with his phone.

His list of names had comments beside each one. Some seemed more likely than others to be important. Ed Thompson from the diner was close to the top of Austin's "trouble" list. Harold Winters, the librarian, had come up in conversation more than once, so Austin added him. The grouchy old men who wouldn't talk to him went on the master list as well as a few more people mentioned in Jamie's notes.

Austin spent an hour online checking through public databases and several more restricted ones. He wasn't sure what he was looking for, but he'd know when he saw it. Frustrated, he pushed the laptop away and grumbled under his breath.

A glance at the time told him it wasn't too late to place a call. After a few rings, someone answered.

"Brent Lawson, Lawson Investigations."

"Brent—hey, it's Austin Williams. From the continuing ed class?"

"Yeah. Hi, Austin. Been a while. What's up?"

"You're going to think I'm crazy—"

"I strongly doubt that."

Austin sighed. "Here goes. I got the feeling when we were talking in the bar that night that you've had a few cases where your clients thought they had a ghost problem."

Brent went quiet long enough that Austin checked to make sure the call hadn't dropped. "Maybe. Why?"

See, this is the crazy part. "The case I'm working on...it's not exactly ghosts. But it requires keeping an open mind."

"How open?" Brent's voice sounded skeptical, wary, and intrigued.

"More about the people who can see ghosts than the ghosts themselves. People who sometimes glimpse things they can't possibly know—or things to come."

"Okay. What's the case?"

Austin blinked, surprised Brent hadn't needed more convincing. "I'm tracking disappearances from a sanitarium in the Adirondacks that happened from the 1960s through the 1980s," he went on. "We think that the patients who vanished might have either been targeted because of their 'something extra' or used it to escape."

"Who's 'we'?"

"My...partner, Jamie. He's a history geek." It felt good to call Jamie his partner, and it sounded more grown-up—and potentially lasting—than boyfriend.

"How the hell did you catch that kind of case?" Brett sounded more worried than angry.

"My grandmother wants to know what happened to her brother so she can die in peace. He'd been at that sanitarium—and vanished."

"Shit. That'll do it." Brett paused. "Okay, start over. How do you think I can help?"

Austin gave him a recap of what they'd learned so far. "I've got five names I'd like to look at more closely."

"Have you researched any of them?" Brent asked.

"I'm in a motel in the wilderness, and the Wi-Fi security is iffy. I'd like to run them through some heavy-duty databases, but I don't want to trust the connection here."

"Gotcha. Gimme the names," Brent said.

Austin gave him the list, spelling each one and giving whatever details he could to help Brent distinguish between people with similar names.

"Okay, that's enough to get me started," Brent said. "What's your end game? The kinds of things that could still be punished after all that time are the worst of the worst— anything less ran through its statute of limitations a long time ago. And we both know the longer it takes, the harder things are to prove."

"Closure," Austin said. "For my grandmother. For the families of the ones who went missing. It's not the kind of thing that's going to go to court. The parties involved are too old—or already dead."

"Watch your back, Austin," Brent warned. "You were a cop. You know how people are. They'll kill to protect their reputations, even if the facts wouldn't send them to jail. And since you brought up ghosts...vengeful spirits aren't anything to fool around with. They can be very dangerous—and they don't always bother to separate the good guys from the bad guys."

Austin knew he'd been right to call Brent. He hadn't confided in Brent about his visions at the conference, but things the other man alluded to gave Austin the feeling he understood—and believed.

"Have you heard about things like this happening—people with abilities going missing?"

Brent sighed. "It's not that uncommon. Sometimes they run away from an abusive situation. In other cases, someone thinks they're doing the world a favor by removing anything supernatural. Those are the easy ones to solve."

An icy knot formed in Austin's stomach. "What are the hard ones?"

"Special people with certain 'talents' command a high price in some circles," Brent said, loathing clear in his voice. "It's one form of trafficking that'll never make the evening news, but it's real."

"Fuck. You know how crazy that sounds?"

Brent snorted. "Yeah, I do. Doesn't make it any less real."

"Okay," Austin replied, letting out a long breath. "I hear you. We'll be careful."

"I'll let you know what I find," Brent promised. "And I've got a hacker friend who can dig into places I can't get to."

Austin ended the call and sat staring out the motel window at the parking lot lights for a few minutes, trying to process what he'd heard.

Brent believes the supernatural stuff is real, and he's been special ops, FBI, and a cop. Hmm. Didn't he tell me at the conference that his boyfriend was an ex-priest? Interesting pairing. Do they hunt this kind of stuff? Does that happen in real life?

A knock at the door startled Austin. Since it was too early for Jamie, he had no reason to expect company. Austin pulled his Sig Sauer out of the waistband holster that let him carry low and hidden at the small of his back. He kept the weapon down as he went to look through the peephole.

Greg from the front desk stood on the stoop, looking nervous.

Austin opened the door cautiously, keeping the gun in hand but out of sight. "Hi, Greg. Something wrong?"

Greg glanced nervously one way and the other. "Can I come in?"

Austin stepped back, still shielding his piece. "What's up?" he asked as Greg moved inside and shut the door.

"You and the new guy at the archive are ruffling feathers about Havenwood," Greg said. "I'm inclined to help you—but first, I want to know what's in it for you."

Austin re-holstered his weapon as discreetly as possible, but he saw Greg track his movement, and he knew the other man understood. "It's a favor to my grandmother. Her brother disappeared from there in 1965. He was fifteen."

"You're not writing an article, are you." Greg didn't even make it a question.

Austin shook his head. "I'm a private investigator. Former cop. Grandma Helen figured I was her last hope to get answers before she passed on. And if family guilt isn't a good reason to do something insane and dangerous, I don't know what is."

Greg chuckled ruefully in agreement. "Ain't that the truth."

"So you said you thought you could help," Austin said, fidgety until he knew Greg's game.

"My uncle was a police detective in Saranac Lake during the 1960s, and he worked the missing persons cases. He couldn't solve some of them. That haunted him, even after he moved to Florida. He died last year, ninety years old," Greg said with clear respect.

"Sorry to hear that."

"He called me not long before he died and told me I was his favorite nephew." Greg chuckled at that. "Then Uncle George said he thought he had solved the Havenwood cases —but that no one would believe him. Even so, he wanted to give me his case files and all his notes. I had to promise not to tell any of the locals, and I had to go down to Florida in person to pick them up."

"What did they say?"

Greg shook his head. "I never looked at them. I guess I didn't want to know things that I couldn't change." He shrugged. "Maybe I was a coward."

Austin shook his head. "You were smart. Knowing would have been dangerous. No shame in protecting yourself."

Greg rubbed the back of his neck. "Okay. If you say so. But if you can do something good with the information, it's yours. I keep thinking about those families who never found out what happened, and they deserve better. Even if the people who did the damage are beyond the reach of the law."

"Thank you," Austin said, surprised at the sudden turn the conversation had taken.

"I'll bring the box over. But I think keeping it secret is still a good idea."

"I agree. I won't blow your cover."

Greg sighed. "That makes me sound like some kind of international spy. I'm definitely not. I run a motel in a tourist town. I leave the action and adventure to guys like you."

Austin snorted. "Trust me, it's not glamorous. But I can let you keep your illusions," he added with a grin.

"I'll be right back." Greg let himself out, and Austin went to pour them both a drink. Greg returned minutes later with a cardboard bankers box and placed it on the table. Austin handed him a drink, and Greg took it, bumping the plastic glasses together with a crinkle instead of a clink.

"To closure," Austin said.

"To justice," Greg answered.

"*Slainte*."

Greg took a sip of the whiskey and nodded his approval. "I still don't want to know."

"In that case, I won't tell you."

Greg shook his head. "You don't understand. I don't *want* to know—but if I *need* to know so I can help, I will."

Austin saw the fear in Greg's eyes and the stubborn set of his jaw. "Thank you."

"If you need a translator for reading Uncle George's handwriting, just holler for me. Trying to 'creatively interpret' the note he'd write in the Christmas card became an ongoing joke in my family," he added with a laugh. "It didn't get better with age. You think doctors have bad penmanship —he would have given them a run for their money."

Austin grinned. "That sounds like a deal." His smile faded. "But I don't want to cause you problems in town. This is your home."

"My family's been here as long as anyone's. I went to school with most of the folks who are in charge now. Not only do I remember who peed their pants in elementary school, I remember some much more 'sensitive' mistakes in high school and our 'wild' twenties. Some things don't have a statute of limitations. Uncle George taught me to always cover my ass."

"I knew there was a reason I liked you."

Greg knocked back the rest of the whiskey and set the cup aside. "Gotta get back up front. Call if you need me."

Austin closed the door behind Greg and locked it. Then he poured himself another drink, opened the box, and settled in. He'd already decided to escort Jamie from the archive to the hotel to keep him safe. Until then, he dug into the files, hoping to unravel the Havenwood mysteries—and maybe, Thomas's fate.

8

JAMIE

J amie gathered the materials he and Austin had been studying and put them in his office. He had the set-up for the event done in less than half an hour, and he knew that neither the speaker nor the attendees were likely to arrive much before the starting time. That gave him a chance to go back through the notes he made from their research that afternoon.

The names he had found linked to Havenwood didn't mean anything to Jamie by themselves. On impulse, he started putting the names into a local genealogy database and paid attention to the descendants. If the parent or grandparent was dead or too old to care about someone stirring up old scandals, their adult children or grandchildren might be more protective.

Jamie hadn't been in Saranac Lake long enough to know a lot of people. Even so, he recognized several of the names of the descendants of the Havenwood workers, including the sheriff, the head librarian, and his boss. That fact alone didn't mean they were involved. Hundreds of people had worked at the hospital over the decades. Only a small number were likely to be active participants in the disappearances. But as Austin had theorized earlier, the others might well have heard rumors. Now that Jamie knew who to look out for, he felt better prepared to protect himself and Austin.

Under normal circumstances, Jamie's preference was to start asking colleagues for advice. Given that everyone he knew in town was potentially compromised by a connection to Havenwood, that option was out.

How about that guy I met at the lecture series last year? The one who wrote ghost books and seemed to know a lot about folklore?

They'd hit it off in a conversation after the program and ended up talking for hours in the hotel bar. Jamie had taken his card, but even more importantly, he had put the man's phone number in his contacts, having an odd suspicion he'd need to contact him one day.

With a glance toward the door to make sure no one was about to head inside, Jamie made up his mind. He dodged into the kitchen and placed the call before he could second guess himself.

"Grand Strand Ghost Tours—this is Simon Kincaide," the man answered.

"Hi, Simon. It's Jamie Miller—I don't know if you remember me. We met at the history conference in Savannah last year."

Simon's response was warm and immediate. "Jamie! Hi! Great to hear from you. Of course I remember you. You're in Rochester, right?" At the conference, he and Simon had talked at length about the difference in weather between Myrtle Beach, where Simon ran a ghost tour shop and worked with the police as a psychic, and Jamie's home in Rochester.

"Actually, I'm in Saranac Lake, temporarily, running a historical association," Jamie replied.

"Good for you. I hope it works out."

Jamie smiled. "I think it just might," he said, thinking of Austin instead of his job. He paused. "Hey, I hate to bother you in the middle of the workday—"

"No bother. How can I help?"

Jamie hadn't quite framed his question before just now, and he realized how crazy it might sound. "In folklore, what kind of creatures prey on young teenagers who are just coming into their powers?"

Simon was quiet for a moment. "That's...oddly specific. Talk to me, Jamie. What's going on?"

Jamie found himself giving Simon a quick recap about the disappearances at Havenwood and the theory that the young people were committed because their abilities manifested. Simon listened in silence, which made Jamie feel simultaneously validated and unsettled.

"Any creature that can leech off the energy of others would be a suspect," Simon replied. "Psi vampires, dark witches, attachment spirits, incubi, succubi, some types of demons...it's a pretty big pool of possibilities."

"Are we talking hypothetically?" Jamie asked.

"If you're asking about real disappearances, and you called with that question, I think you know the answer," Simon replied.

"Can the creatures pass for human?" Jamie's heartbeat raced.

"Some can. But there's another possible explanation that's simpler—humans who want to capture and control those with powers for their own purposes."

Jamie swallowed hard. "That's a thing?"

"Unfortunately, yes. In fact, there was a problem up your

way just a few months ago. A Huntsman was going after special people because wealthy clients *wanted* them."

Simon didn't define "wanted for what reason," and Jamie didn't ask. All of a sudden, he had the sense that maybe Simon knew about a much bigger, darker, scarier world than Jamie had ever glimpsed, far beyond the ability to see ghosts.

"How would we know which sort we were dealing with?" Jamie asked, glad his voice sounded steady.

"You won't until you're in the thick of it." Simon paused. "Jamie, you and Austin don't have to handle this. There are people—hunters—who protect people from things that go bump in the night."

I'm gonna file that little fact away to think about later. I thought those TV shows were just fiction.

"This is personal for Austin. He's not going to back off—and I promised to support him."

Simon sighed. "I figured you'd say that. Alright, how about this—you and Austin figure out who's behind the disappearances and call me back. We can get someone up there to handle the dangerous part. Austin gets closure, and neither of you end up dead."

"I like the part about not being dead," Jamie replied.

"Have your ghosts had anything to say about this situation?"

Jamie had found himself trusting Simon easily during their long conversation at the conference and had admitted his ability to see spirits.

"Does dropping a portfolio of floor plans on my head count?"

"I'd say so," Simon answered and chuckled. "Try asking them questions. Maybe they'll answer."

Jamie wasn't sure how much the ghosts at the association knew about Havenwood, but maybe the spirit who nudged the floor plan folio off the shelf was bound to one of the boxes for the exhibit and not to the repurposed house.

"I'll give it a go," he said, thinking that there were certain to be spirits at the hospital. He figured that mentioning the expedition he and Austin were planning probably wouldn't go over well with Simon, so he didn't say anything.

"Be careful, Jamie. Whether it's people or some kind of supernatural creature, they don't want their secret to get out. That makes them dangerous."

Simon gave Jamie a shortlist of protective items. Salt, iron, silver, and holy water wouldn't be hard to get, and if it would help keep them safe while they investigated, Jamie figured it was worth the effort.

We've got a canister of salt in the kitchen here. I have to go back to my apartment to pack a bag—there's a fireplace poker I can take with me. As for silver...I've got a couple of saints' medallion necklaces I haven't worn in a long time. The holy water's tougher, but maybe I can get Austin to stop at a church early in the morning. Assuming he doesn't laugh his ass off when I tell him.

Jamie thanked Simon and promised to keep him updated. Then he went to the front door, flipped the lock and the *Back in an Hour* sign, and headed to the second floor.

"I don't know which one of you helped me find the floor plans to Havenwood Hospital, but thank you," he said aloud in the storage room. "Austin and I are trying to find out what happened to the people who disappeared from the hospital. If you know anything and you can help us, I'd really appreciate it."

He waited for a few minutes, unsure what kind of response he might receive. The room felt colder than usual, and a prickle on the back of his neck told him that *something* was listening.

Nothing stirred. No boxes tipped or pages ruffled. Jamie wasn't sure exactly what he'd been expecting, but he had hoped to get some sort of reaction.

"Just think about it, okay?" he added, wondering if the ghosts were present but outside his ability to see.

Jamie hadn't gotten through all of the "Through Their Eyes" memory boxes yet, since the public response had been enthusiastic and his predecessor had let the backlog grow. Havenwood had been a big area employer back in the day. Surely there were more former employees among the people whose memories were contained in those boxes. Maybe they had seen things they didn't understand at the time, didn't know how to stop, or they'd been afraid to intervene. Lending a hand now could still help the grieving families of the vanished patients find peace and expose the people who hurt them for some measure of justice.

He felt his phone buzz a warning about the time and hurried downstairs, remembering to unlock the door and flip the sign back to *Open*. Moments later, the chime sounded, and Jamie walked out of the break room to find his boss surveying the set-up for the night's event.

"Looks good," he said. "You got a confirmation from the speaker?"

Jamie nodded. "Talked to him, not just email. He'll be here. And Mr. Quincey dropped off the cookies. I was just heading back to make the trays for afterward."

Donovan Andrews's successful career in real estate made him a local fixture in the business community and a wealthy man. He was a board member of several non-profits, including the Historical Association, so when Jamie's predecessor died, it fell to Donovan to find a replacement.

Jamie hadn't been entirely comfortable with Andrews during his interviews. Something about the man struck him as false, although he didn't think Andrews was actually lying. At the time, Andrews had pitched the temporary role to Jamie as necessary because he felt the organization needed the permanent archivist to have deep area roots to cultivate donors and support. Now that Jamie knew Andrews's family had Havenwood connections, he wondered if his boss wasn't also looking for someone complicit by blood who wouldn't dig up old dirt.

"Jamie, if I could have a word before you head back to the kitchen."

Donovan's voice took on a tone Jamie remembered from school, usually right before being given detention. He felt his heart rate kick up and tried not to freeze like a deer in the headlights.

"Of course," he said, proud that his voice sounded steady.

"I know you're new in town, and you haven't even had much of a chance to settle in," Donovan said, framing what Jamie had always called a "shit sandwich"—say something nice, criticize, and then say something else nice. *I bet he learned that in one of those management books.*

"And I know you have the training to be a historian, and that's your passion. But...for the short time you're here, I think the best use of your time is keeping the archive up and running and working through whatever Richard left undone."

"I'm not sure I understand," Jamie replied, although he was totally certain he did.

"A few people have taken me aside and let me know that you've been asking questions about a rather delicate period in our town's history," Andrews said with a smile so fake it reminded Jamie of his sister's Ken doll. "Havenwood Hospital was a product of its times. It did a lot of good work, helped many vulnerable individuals, and provided employment to quite a few local residents. Like any organization, it made mistakes, but there's nothing to be gained at this point by poking at things that might or might not have happened decades ago." Andrews's words were so smooth they had to have been rehearsed.

Jamie could be a pretty good actor when the situation called for it, despite the way his heart pounded from the implied threat. "I'm sorry—I didn't mean anything by it. I just found some comments in old papers I was filing and was curious. I hope that didn't cause any trouble."

"Of course not," Andrews assured him, and Jamie knew it was a blatant lie.

Jamie's smile held firm. "I'm glad you told me. I certainly don't want to make any waves."

"I knew you'd understand," Andrews replied. "There's an out-of-towner who's been upsetting some of the older people in the community, poking his nose into things, making accusations. We can't afford to have the archive associated with that sort of thing."

"Of course not." *With luck, I'll be sleeping with that out-of-towner tonight.*

"Well then, that's settled. I'm glad we had this little talk. Keep up the good work." Andrews patted Jamie on the shoulder and left as Jamie stared after him.

He sounds like every bad TV boss ever. I knew when I interviewed with him that he was going to be a pain in my ass. Then again, if I hadn't taken the job, I wouldn't have met Austin. Totally worth it.

Shit. I need to get the cookies ready.

Jamie ran to the break room, glad that he'd already

started to set out paper plates, foam cups, napkins, and the powdered sugar and creamer needed for coffee. Quincey had said he'd be back to make coffee, so Jamie made sure the coffee maker was clean and put the ground coffee and a filter next to it. He set out the cookies on two trays and breathed a sigh of relief.

The door chimed again, and Jamie headed back to the main room as Quincey and the speaker came in together. Quincey was excitedly asking questions, and the speaker looked a tad overwhelmed.

"Mr. Quincey! I've got everything ready for you in the break room," Jamie hailed the older man, hoping to give the speaker a reprieve. He hurried to welcome their guest and spent the next few minutes in a flurry of activity as the night's attendees slowly trickled in.

"Please find a seat," Jamie called to them. "And don't forget to stop in the break room for coffee and cookies afterward!"

———

BY THE TIME Jamie finally herded the last of the attendees out of the door, each with a doggy bag of cookies, it was close to eleven. He had been trying since ten to politely get them to shove off and noted jealously that the speaker had slipped out unnoticed not long after the presentation.

He locked the door with a sigh of relief. The chairs were already put away—a not-too-subtle hint that had been completely ignored. Quincey and his five friends had chatted while Jamie cleaned up the coffee maker and put away the rest of the materials.

Jamie texted Austin to let him know he'd be late since he still needed to stop by his place to pick up a change of clothing. He hurried through his checklist to shut the archive down for the night and felt relieved that the ghosts were fairly quiet. *Maybe they liked listening in while the old guys were talking.*

As Jamie passed the stairs to the second floor, he heard a thump in the storage room. Remembering that he'd asked the ghosts for help, Jamie pushed down his nervousness and went upstairs to see what was going on.

He hesitated before opening the door, then took a deep breath, flicked on the light, and stepped inside.

Jamie had expected to find books or something else on the floor, given the thump he'd heard. To his surprise, nothing was out of place. Jamie looked all around before he saw it.

Safe.

The word had been scratched into the plaster wall, deep gouges that hadn't been present before.

"I don't understand," he said to the empty room. "Are the missing people safe? Are Austin and I safe? Who's safe? And who are we safe from?"

Only silence answered him. "Okay," Jamie said. "Sleep on it, and maybe you can fill me in tomorrow."

He headed back downstairs, activated the alarm, locked the door, and headed out. The quiet night left him with his thoughts, and he had too many questions.

To his surprise, Jamie found Austin lounging beside his car.

"I didn't know you were going to drive," Austin said with a shrug. "So I thought if you had to walk, I'd walk with you."

"How long have you been out here? It's freezing."

"Not too long. You can help me warm up later," Austin said with a grin.

"Hope you don't mind, but I need to make a couple of stops. I'll fill you in on the way."

On the drive, Jamie saw lights up ahead, and he slowed and pulled over to the curb. Our Lady of the Snows Catholic Church was lit up to welcome parishioners, and the sign outside advertised a midnight mass.

"Wait here—I'll be right back." Jamie stepped to one side, dumped out the contents of his refillable water bottle, and slipped into the church. Since it was only eleven-thirty, most parishioners hadn't arrived, and the priest was busy elsewhere. Jamie sidled up to the font and quickly filled his bottle, then left before anyone noticed.

Holy water was easier to get than I expected.

When they reached his duplex, Austin swore when he saw the screen door that had been sliced open.

"Leave it to the landlord," Jamie said. "Come on inside—I'll pack quick."

"Bring enough for a couple of days," Austin said, managing to look protective and hopeful at the same time. "I think it would be good for us to stick together."

Despite the circumstances, the thought warmed Jamie's heart. Austin stayed on guard in the kitchen while Jamie grabbed sleep pants as well as several outfits, his shaving kit, and the items Simon had recommended to protect them against ghosts. He also took his laptop, eBook reader and chargers, and threw his good watch, gaming console, and passport into his duffel, just in case the vandals decided to break in. That didn't leave much to steal that didn't belong to the landlord. He was still mostly living out of boxes since he hadn't bothered to completely unpack.

A quick look around assured him that he hadn't forgotten anything important, then he headed back to the kitchen where Austin waited. Despite everything, Jamie hoped the day would have a happy ending.

Austin met him with a warm smile and a hot kiss. "I forgot to ask—how'd everything go at the event?"

Jamie kissed him back and squeezed Austin's ass to make it clear how much he was missed, waiting to reply until he'd locked up the duplex and they were back in his car.

"Long. Boring. And the guests wouldn't leave as long as we had cookies left, so I had to give them all to-go bags."

Austin laughed. "That's okay. We're together now."

Jamie parked beside Austin's 4Runner and grabbed his bag out of the back.

Austin opened the door and ushered him in with a sweep of his arm. "I'd offer to give you the grand tour, but it's a motel room. What you see is what you get."

He motioned toward the table. "I didn't know if you'd be hungry, so I've got chips and salsa and some other snacks."

"I'm starving," Jamie admitted. Then he took a look at the room and froze. "Is that a... moose?" He pointed at the huge stuffed, antlered head on the wall, its face covered by a bath towel. Jamie slowly took in the decor. "Wow. So many moose. Mooses?"

"Each room has a theme," Austin told him, straight-faced. "It could be worse."

"Yeah," Jamie murmured. "Actually, it could. I stayed at a hotel once that had red plastic emperor penguins, and they moved them around every day—in the hallways, even in the guest rooms. You'd come around a corner and, wham! There was a penguin that wasn't there the day before." He shivered. "I haven't trusted penguins since. Shifty bastards."

Jamie gave the moose head one more suspicious glare, then started snacking while Austin grabbed beer from the small fridge.

"You're infamous," he told Austin once he pushed the chips away. "My boss thinks you're a bad influence."

"Your boss?" Austin brought two more beers, and they both sat at the table. "Tell me."

Jamie rolled his eyes, second-guessing his decision to say anything. He didn't want Austin to back off out of a misplaced desire to protect him. "He's an entitled prick. I knew it when I took the job, but I didn't care because it wasn't meant to last long. He's also related to half the town, and he had family involved with Havenwood."

"So he's invested in keeping things quiet."

Jamie nodded. This wasn't going the way he'd planned. He wanted to enjoy his time with Austin, not drag down the mood. After all, he'd been looking forward all day to getting it up.

"I'm pretty sure he hired me because I was young, and he thought I'd be easy to control," Jamie replied with a sigh. "Maybe he figured that anyone with a Ph.D. who would take a temporary position wouldn't be ambitious enough to cause trouble."

"Fuck him and the horse he rode in on," Austin snapped, rising to Jamie's defense. "That's a load of bullshit."

"Truly ambitious people don't spend years getting a graduate degree on the Victorian Era," Jamie said with a self-deprecating smile. "Not gonna get me a corner office."

"Truly ambitious people don't become private investigators either," Austin said, bumping shoulders with him in solidarity. "It took you plenty of ambition to finish your degree. Just like it did for me to make it through the police academy. Sometimes the road just takes a few turns you didn't expect."

"I don't care about Andrews's opinion. I'm happy with what I studied. I figure I'll find the right job sooner or later, and in the meantime, coming here meant I met you." He leaned forward and kissed Austin, tasting beer on his lips.

"My point was, be careful. It sounds like word is getting around that we're flipping over rocks and seeing what crawls out from under. They might start making things uncomfortable."

Austin laid a hand on Jamie's thigh. "Message received."

"But I did get some advice on how to be a little safer." Jamie filled him in on his call to Simon and patted his backpack. "I brought all the stuff Simon mentioned. Figured it couldn't hurt to take it with us."

"I'm impressed."

The look in Austin's eyes made it clear he meant what he said. That warmed Jamie to his core. "Thanks."

"You want to watch a movie or something? Let you wind down a bit?" Austin asked as he picked up the empty beer bottles and rolled the snack bags closed.

Jamie covered Austin's hand with his own. "It's late, and we wanted to head over to Havenwood early. And to be honest, I had a few other ideas about how to relax."

"I like how you think."

———

THEY'D SUCKED each other off before going to sleep, cozy and completely spent. Jamie woke Austin with a morning wood blow job, and Austin had stroked him off in the shower, warm and wet against Jamie's back, starting to chub up again pressed into the crack of Jamie's ass.

With both of them in their thirties, they might not bounce back quite as fast as a decade earlier, but Jamie knew if they ever got the chance to spend a day in bed, he would enjoy the hell out of the in-between times, kissing and touching, mapping out his lover's body with his eyes and hands and tongue.

"I thought we might want to get out of town without attracting attention, so I bought breakfast stuff last night if you don't mind coffee and muffins," Austin said. "We don't need anyone deciding to follow us."

Jamie mumbled his agreement around the muffin he was already eating, then washed it down with coffee.

"I've got the floor plans on my phone," Austin said.

"Me too."

"Good. Even so, let's make sure we don't get separated," Austin warned.

Jamie nodded and then unloaded a few things from his backpack. He set the clean clothing on the bed next to his sleep pants and shaving kit, leaving the protective items Simon had recommended in the pack.

Jamie watched Austin check the clip on his handgun and slip it into a holster along his back. "I'm bringing some protection of my own—in case ghosts aren't the only thing we have to worry about."

They drove Austin's SUV out to the site of the old hospital. On the drive, Austin fidgeted, and Jamie watched him, wondering what was wrong.

"You're going to think I'm nuts," Austin said. "Remember when I asked you if there was a strange new shop near your apartment? When I was coming back from your place at midnight a couple of nights ago, there was a store still open and all lit up. Called itself a 'magic emporium.' I thought it might be some sort of escape room or role-playing adventure. It looked like a store out of Harry Potter or Lord of the Rings—I'm not kidding."

Jamie frowned. "I haven't seen anything like that. I'd

have remembered. Hell, I'd probably be their best customer."

Austin looked uncomfortable, like he was expecting Jamie to laugh or doubt his word. Jamie reached over and laid his hand on Austin's thigh. "Whatever you saw, I'll believe you. I've seen some strange things myself."

Austin let out a long breath. "Thanks. You might want take-backs on that promise when you hear me out." He told Jamie about the odd "save-me sack," unusual clerk, and the bigger-on-the-inside store filled with items that sounded like they belonged in the prop room for a fantasy movie.

"And after all that, when we opened the box, all it had in it was a piece of paper with six numbers written on it." Austin shook his head as if he had trouble believing the tale himself. "I'd think I imagined it all, but the paper is still in my wallet."

"With that kind of build-up, it should have been a dragon scale or a wyvern tooth, or an amulet that gives you some kind of cool magic," Jamie agreed. "If that was a video game and I'd fought a bunch of murderous leeches to get that box, I'd be kinda pissed to get a piece of paper for all my trouble."

Austin grinned. "Murderous leeches?"

Jamie shrugged. "It was a very swampy dungeon. But we digress. Tell me more."

Austin relaxed, realizing that Jamie wasn't going to make fun of him or write off his strange experience. Jamie squeezed his thigh in reassurance.

"The next day, the store wasn't just gone—it was like it had never been there," Austin said. "The building wasn't big enough to contain the huge place I walked through. The folks at the donut place said it had been vacant for years. But I swear what happened to me was real. And now

I can't stop wondering what those numbers on the paper mean."

Jamie frowned, thinking. "How about a patient ID or a case identifier? An account number? The code for a security system? What else uses numbers?"

"That's the problem," Austin said. "There are so many possibilities, and without something to connect the numbers to, I don't know how to start. But assuming what I saw was real—then I'm going to have a 'dire need' for that number. What if I can't figure it out in time, and I can't use the code to protect us?"

Austin's voice and expression made his distress clear. Jamie could see how much the odd encounter bothered his partner and how important it was to him to keep them both safe. "We'll make sense of it," Jamie promised. "If we put our heads together, I'm sure we'll find the answer." He smirked. "I'm always in favor of putting our *heads* together."

His cheesy joke seemed to lighten Austin's mood, and Austin dropped one hand from the steering wheel to cover Jamie's. "Thank you. I was really afraid you'd write me off as a nutcase."

"I'm going to be an adult and not make any jokes right now about your nuts," Jamie replied, figuring that they could both use a moment to lighten the tension. "I certainly can't explain what you encountered, but I don't doubt you experienced it. I believe you. Strange things happen. And if these disappearances happened because the patients had supernatural abilities...well, a freaky wizard store isn't much of a stretch, is it?"

Austin's smile in response made Jamie's heart swell with affection. "You're amazing," Austin said, and while he kept his eyes on the road, Jamie could hear the fondness in his tone.

"Right back atcha," Jamie replied, keeping the mood light, although Austin's words warmed him, making him hope that once the case was finished, they could be so much more to each other than a vacation fling.

———

JAMIE FOUND an access driveway that got them close to the fence without needing to leave the car where it could be seen from the main road. Even so, Austin parked off to the side beneath the trees.

"We'll have to hike in from here," Austin said.

Jamie shouldered his pack, and Austin grabbed a small duffel out of the back seat. He unzipped it and tossed a canister of pepper spray to Jamie.

"If there are animals or squatters, this'll help you get out without having to do real harm," he explained as he zipped the pack back up. "I've got several regular flashlights and a heavy-duty jacklight, plus batteries and some other useful odds and ends. Just in case." Jamie made sure they each wore a silver amulet, and he carried his pack with the protective items. Austin checked his gun and then slid it back into his holster.

Havenwood sprawled across the ridge of a hill, imposing and ominous. Jamie had seen enough horror movies to expect bad things from such a place and had read enough history to know that reality could be worse.

"The architecture was amazing," Austin said as they walked along the chain-link fence, looking for an opening. "The planners had good ideas—enlightened for their time. But the people who got hired to carry out the work caused a lot of pain."

"Cue the scary music," Jamie replied.

"No kidding. This is the part of the movie when you wonder what the hell the characters think they're doing."

Jamie felt a little better when he heard a note of tension in Austin's voice, which reassured him that he wasn't the only one on edge. The hospital had been abandoned for decades. He'd watched plenty of urban exploration videos —old buildings could be plenty dangerous even without ghosts and an evil past.

"What are we looking for?" Jamie asked.

Austin shook his head. "I don't know. Anything of value would have been removed or stolen long ago, so I don't think they just left files lying around for us to find. Maybe once we see the layout, we can figure out how Huffman and his helpers could have made so many people disappear without being seen."

The front doors were chained shut, but the lock on a side door had been picked long ago, given the scratches around the keyhole. It sat ajar, making Jamie wonder whether the site had any security patrols or had just been left on its own.

Inside, the cold, damp air made Jamie shiver. "Between the dust and the mold, this isn't going to do my allergies any favors."

"I don't plan to stay long," Austin assured him.

They emerged from the side corridor into the main section. Sunlight streamed through the huge, dirty windows, illuminating the big entrance hall. Jamie remembered reading that having plenty of windows was an intentional change from the dungeon-like hospitals of the past. Even so, they didn't wholly repel the gloom.

Once, the foyer had been airy and impressive. Between the large windows, white walls, and the open atrium, the entrance would have been bright, welcoming, and filled with sunlight—an implied promise to restore health and sanity.

Now, paint peeled from the plaster walls in long gray strips. A thick layer of dust covered everything, and Jamie didn't want to think too much about its composition. A building this old surely contained multiple biohazards. *Probably one of the reasons it hasn't been redeveloped. Expensive as hell to clean up.* Where windows were cracked or broken, dirt and leaves had blown in, settling into corners. The building wasn't tight enough to keep out animals, but anything nesting here stayed hidden. Jamie didn't want to think about what might be living in the walls.

He felt the hair on the back of his neck stand up, and Jamie knew the ghosts of Havenwood were watching them. Fear tightened his belly, and he wasn't sure which he was more afraid of—encountering the spirits or confessing his ability to Austin.

"Huffman's office was on the second floor," Austin whispered, even though they were alone. Jamie understood. The old hospital freaked him out. "The main stairs look solid, but watch your step." A wide, open stairwell curved up from the main foyer, looking more like a grand hotel or mansion than a mental hospital.

Austin led the way, and Jamie realized that his partner gripped the heavy flashlight like a weapon, so he guessed he wasn't the only one on edge. At the top of the stairs, a long hallway stretched in both directions, spanning the length of the large main building. Double doors at both ends marked the entrances to the wings on either side.

"The offices and treatment areas were in this building," Austin said, keeping his voice low even though nothing suggested that the abandoned hospital had been recently disturbed. "The wings were residential, for live-in staff as well as patients."

Jamie remembered the plans they'd studied. Two basements lay beneath the building. The first level had the laundry facility and the morgue, and the mechanical room took up most of the sub-basement, along with storage. Given the way the hospital sat on the ridge, what was below ground at the front of the building opened on ground-level at the rear.

Huffman's office was most of the way down the right-hand corridor. The farther they went from the main atrium, the darker the hallway became since the closed office doors blocked the light from the windows.

Austin stopped in the middle of the hallway, and Jamie saw him tense up. He looked ready for a fight, but Jamie hadn't seen anything worrisome. Even the ghosts seemed to be keeping their distance.

"Austin—what's wrong?"

Austin shook his head and turned, giving Jamie a reassuring smile that didn't reach his eyes. "Nothing. Just—weird moment of déja vu."

He led them to Room 217, Huffman's office. The door opened easily, brighter inside from windows that took up most of the far wall.

"I'm always surprised at the stuff they leave behind in these kind of places," Austin muttered as they looked around. A steel desk, painted institutional-green, sat in front of the windows. Filing cabinets with their drawers pulled out lined another wall. On the right-hand wall, two bookshelves covered most of the space. A quick check showed everything to be empty.

"Now what?" Jamie asked.

Austin shook his head. "I'm not sure. I hoped that we'd find an important clue—"

He broke off speaking with a moan of pain and staggered, dropping the flashlight and gripping his temples with both hands.

"Austin? Are you okay? What's happening?"

Jamie ran to him and shoved his flashlight into his belt so he could hold onto Austin by his forearms. "Austin?" he repeated, shaking the other man to rouse him.

Austin's eyes were glassy and unfocused. His face looked pinched and pale, and he hunched over with his arms wrapped around himself like he was in pain.

"Austin—you're scaring me." Jamie could feel the ghosts drawing closer, curious about the new trespassers. The room grew colder. Jamie caught motion out of the corner of his eye and glimpses of gray shadows not caused by the daylight. He put himself between Austin and where he felt the ghosts' presence most strongly, protecting his partner.

"We mean you no harm," Jamie said to the ghosts since it didn't look like he'd be getting Austin to move quickly. "The bad man who worked here—we want to find out what happened to the people he took away, try to help their families. Please don't hurt us. I'm just trying to keep my partner safe."

A breeze stirred, but the windows here weren't cracked. Jamie turned to follow another blur of motion, and when he looked again, the word "safe" had been drawn in the window grime. He knew for certain that it hadn't been there when they entered.

"Can you walk, Austin? We need to get out of here." Jamie felt no malice from the spirits near them. But when he concentrated, he sensed that there were more restless ghosts elsewhere in the hospital, and he knew in his gut they were dangerous.

"Yeah," Austin said, sounding like he was coming up for air after a deep dive underwater. "I'm okay."

No, you're not, Jamie thought, but now wasn't the time to argue.

"We're leaving," Jamie said to the ghosts. "Please help us get out safely."

In the distance, he felt the angry spirits brewing like a storm in the offing. He didn't doubt that the revenants were entitled to their rage, that they'd been betrayed and abused. He just didn't want to have to fight their way out, especially with Austin injured.

"Come on," he said to Austin and bent down to pick up the dropped flashlight. Jamie slipped an arm around his waist and guided him back the way they came. They took the stairs at a careful pace, but by the time they reached the bottom, Austin seemed more himself.

"Hurry." Jamie felt the conflicting energies between the angry ghosts and the protective spirits throbbing in his temples. He manhandled Austin out the door and half-dragged him across the lawn to the fence, then shoved him through the cut in the chain-link. Once they crossed the steel barrier, the pain in his head eased, then vanished.

A loud *bang* sounded as they neared the 4Runner. Austin dropped to the ground, pulling Jamie down, and rolled on top of him, reaching for his gun.

"What the—" Jamie started.

"Shh!" Austin shifted his weight to the side so Jamie could breathe but still kept him pinned. "Stay down," he hissed. He scrambled to a crouch and gestured for Jamie not to move. Gun in hand and staying low, Austin reached up to angle the side mirror, looking for the shooter.

"There's a small cement block building a little ways down the road," Austin whispered. "I think the shooter was on the roof." He still looked like crap, but it was obvious to Jamie that Austin's police training had kicked in. Everything about him had turned watchful and wary, with an undercurrent of danger Jamie knew he'd find sexy once they weren't being shot at.

"Do you see anyone?" Jamie kept his voice low.

Austin shook his head. He was still pale, not entirely steady on his feet.

"Give me the keys. I'll drive," Jamie demanded.

Austin hesitated, then handed them over. They both crawled in through the passenger door, keeping their heads below the windows. Jamie slid down in the driver's seat as low as he could and still see over the dash, an advantage of being the shorter of the two of them.

Jamie shoved down his worry and peeled out, flooring it until they were past the utility building and out of range, leaving a cloud of dust behind them. His heart pounded, and his hands were sweating in their vise grip on the steering wheel. When he finally dared to sit up, he swallowed hard to fight the urge to throw up.

"Someone shot at us!" he yelped, slowing down only when he reached the main road.

"Yeah," Austin replied, still sounding ill. "With a rifle. Took as much skill to miss us as it would have to hit us. That was a warning."

"How did someone know where we were?" Jamie's voice was higher than his usual tone. "I didn't see anyone following us—did you?"

Austin shook his head. "No. But to an extent, all pickup trucks look alike."

Neither man spoke again until they were in the parking lot.

"Who were you talking to, back at the asylum?" Austin looked more like himself now, although the pinch of his eyebrows suggested the pain wasn't gone.

"I'll tell you everything—and I've got questions of my own," Jamie said. "But first, let's get inside and order dinner."

He slipped his backpack over his right shoulder and steadied Austin with his left arm around his partner's waist. Austin managed to work the room key, and they staggered through the doorway.

"Go lie down. I'll order pizza," Jamie said and worried when Austin did as he was told without protest, stretching out on his back across the bed, knees bent at the end of the mattress, boots on the floor.

He called his favorite pizza place from speed dial and then made sure the door was locked before heading to the bathroom to soak a cloth in cold water and wring it out.

"Here. It'll probably feel good." Jamie handed the cloth to Austin to put over his eyes. He dug a bottle of Advil out of his backpack, found two plastic cups and filled them, and set out tablets for both of them. "Take these. They'll help."

Both men avoided talking until the pizza came. Jamie paid for it over Austin's protests. Austin made his way to the table, and they ate straight from the box, grateful for the napkins in the bag with their sodas.

"You asked someone to protect us, back at Havenwood," Austin said when they had finished off all the slices. "Who were you talking to?" His color had improved, and his eyes weren't narrowed with pain.

Jamie felt a whole different kind of fear than at the

asylum. *Austin believes that the supernatural is real. But will he want a ghost whisperer for a boyfriend?*

"The ghosts," Jamie said. "The ones in the room with us were curious. They didn't want to hurt us. The other ones... elsewhere in the building...were angry. I was afraid they would come after us. So I asked for help."

Austin looked at him for a moment, assessing. Jamie felt his heart in his throat. "That's kinda awesome," Austin said. "Have you been able to do it all your life?"

Jamie felt dizzy with relief. *He's not freaking out.* "I've always seen ghosts. It got stronger once I hit puberty. I can't usually hear them, or make them come to me, or control them. Nothing like that," he hurried to add.

Austin nodded. "That makes sense." He paused, and Jamie could see a struggle in the other man's expression. He stayed silent, waiting for whatever Austin needed to say.

"I get flashes," Austin said. "Visions, I guess, although they aren't like watching a movie. More like clicking the remote too fast and just seeing a series of images but not usually enough to know what they mean."

"And that's what happened in Huffman's office?"

Austin nodded.

"You've had them before, about this case?"

Austin looked up and met Jamie's gaze with a worried look. "Yes. A couple of times before I came to Saranac Lake. Those were different. They were about you."

Jamie's eyebrows rose. "Me?" He thought for a moment. "That's why you reacted the way you did, that first day at the Historical Association. You recognized me."

"Yes." Austin sighed. "In those visions, you were in danger. Now that I've been inside the asylum, I think what I saw happens there."

"Like what we did right now?"

Austin shook his head. 'No. But the long corridor upstairs looked familiar. I think it's the one from my vision. I shouldn't have taken you with me—I put you in danger."

"I wasn't going to let you go alone." Jamie gave his most stubborn expression. "Tell me what you saw this time."

"I saw a woman in an old-fashioned nurse's uniform going into a small room. There were bookshelves and filing cabinets. She went to a green box and took out a file, and held it out to me. That's all."

"It hurts when you get visions?"

"Sometimes," Austin replied. "Like my head might explode."

"I hope that doesn't happen a lot."

Austin managed a wan smile. "Not usually." He grew serious and studied Jamie's face. "Why didn't you tell me about the ghosts?"

"Probably for the same reason you didn't mention the visions," Jamie replied. "I didn't want you to see me different-ly." *I didn't want you to leave.*

Austin reached for Jamie's hand, lacing their fingers together. "I care about you," he admitted. "Learning some-thing new isn't going to change that—especially since I've also got some hidden talents."

"I care about you too," Jamie said quietly. "You scared me to death back there. I didn't know if I could get you out before the bad ghosts came for us."

"But you did." Austin's voice warmed with approval.

"This time."

Jamie was quiet for a moment. "The ghosts wrote a word on the window. 'Safe.' It's the same word they scratched into the plaster in the storage room at the archive." He paused. "I don't know whether we're safe *from* something or need to make someone *else* safe—ghosts are too damn tight-lipped."

Austin got up and carried the empty pizza box to the trash, then brought them both beer, popping off the caps before setting the bottles on the table. "I think we deserve a drink."

He sat across from Jamie and took his hand again. "I had all kinds of ideas about what we might get up to tonight," he said, stroking his thumb over the back of Jamie's hand. Jamie felt a flush, and Austin's low growl went right to his cock. "I'm not sure either of us is in any shape for what I had in mind, but I want a rain check."

He chuckled. "I even bought wine and whiskey, thinking we'd celebrate a win tonight."

"We did. We're still alive."

Austin raised his bottle in a salute and leaned in to kiss Jamie. "Then here's to surviving."

9

AUSTIN

Waking up with Jamie in his arms made Austin happy. Half-asleep, cozy beneath the blankets, almost too warm the way they were spooned together—he knew he could get used to this.

I want to keep him.

He'd thought about seeing if they could make their attraction last, but this was the first time his mind just blurted out the truth. Austin had known from the beginning that Jamie wasn't a one-night stand. By their second dinner together, he realized they were a better fit than nearly all of his past boyfriends.

I'm falling for him.

Jamie stirred, still asleep, made an adorable snuffling noise, and turned to bury his face in Austin's shoulder. Austin raised a hand to comb through Jamie's dark hair, adding a light scalp massage, and Jamie smiled as he leaned into the touch.

"I like mornings with you," Jamie murmured, his voice still rough with sleep. He slipped Austin's thigh between his legs and rubbed up and down, his erection unmistakable through the sleep pants.

"I like waking up with you too." Austin rolled to the side, pushed down both their pants and took both stiff cocks in hand. Jamie kissed him, and they made out like teenagers. Jamie wrapped his hand around Austin's, and their mingled pre-come slicked the way, bringing them both off. Austin's orgasm wasn't the most intense he'd ever had, but he relaxed into a sleepy contentment that more than made up for the lack of mind-blowing fireworks.

"You need to get to work," Austin said reluctantly once the afterglow had worn off.

Jamie whined playfully, but the reluctance in his eyes was real. "I'm comfy."

"So am I. But we've both got stuff to do. How about we plan on dinner and then come back here again...if you still want to."

Jamie kissed him, warm and promising. "I'd like that. Was counting on it, if you want to know the truth."

Does he want this as much as I do? Could we make it work?

"Go take a shower, and I'll make coffee," Austin said. "Since your job has an actual starting time."

Jamie climbed out of bed, and Austin gave his bare ass a playful slap. Jamie wiggled in response, and only extreme self-control kept Austin from pulling him back into bed and giving them both a late start to the day.

Once Jamie headed into the bathroom, Austin went to the small kitchenette and got coffee brewing. He laid out muffins and donuts along with napkins and set creamer and sweetener beside a cup for Jamie.

Austin eyed the banker's box beneath the table, his day's work. He had started to organize the contents, but that required learning George's cramped handwriting, and to an extent, figuring out how he thought. Today, Austin hoped to make more progress, especially if the details he and Jamie had found dovetailed with George's research.

"Coffee smells good," Jamie said as he came out from the bathroom with a towel slung low around his hips. Austin paused to admire the sight and to let Jamie see him appreciating the view. Jamie blushed adorably.

"I'll get my shower once you've headed to work," Austin said, not wanting to waste any of their time together.

Jamie dressed quickly and joined him at the table. They made quick work of the pastries, and Austin resolved to pick up more when he went out for supplies.

"Today should be quiet," Jamie said, licking off the flakes of glaze from his lips. "I'm making good progress on all the 'memory' boxes—not just looking for anything about Havenwood, but getting them logged into the system. Maybe someone can put the exhibit together. I think it would be amazing. And I'll have to do something about the word the ghosts scrawled."

"I may have to take Greg up on his offer to help decipher his uncle's handwriting," Austin said, already pouring himself a second cup. "It doesn't help that the ink's faded, and I suspect Uncle George's hands trembled. That makes it challenging."

Jamie tossed his napkin and cup into the trash, then leaned over to give Austin a lingering kiss. "I'll see you tonight," he promised. "Text me if you get bored. You know the archive isn't a hotbed of excitement. I'll make sure I have my phone on me."

"Sounds like a plan," Austin agreed. He sobered. "Jamie —be careful. Word's obviously gotten around you and I have been poking into old scandals. There might be even more people than we know who don't like the idea."

"I think I'll be safe at work," Jamie said. "It's a public place, in broad daylight."

"Take your car—please don't walk," Austin said. "I'll come by at closing time."

"So it's safe for you to walk, but not me?" Jamie's tone lightened a serious question.

"I've been a cop and a detective," Austin reminded him. "I trained for dicey situations. And I've got a gun."

Jamie leaned over Austin, who was still sitting at the table and hugged his shoulders from behind. "I'll take care. You too."

Austin walked him to the door and kissed him, soft with a bit of heat behind it, then waved goodbye. He waited until Jamie got into his car safely and drove away before he went back inside. After he locked the door, Austin grabbed a refill of coffee and settled back at the table, spreading out documents to cover the entire surface.

That lasted until Housekeeping changed the sheets and brought fresh towels. Then Austin put the *Do Not Disturb* hanger on the doorknob, closed the curtains, turned on all the lights, and pulled out a roll of blue painter's tape from his bag. He dragged the table closer to the bed and spread out the rest of the materials from George's box across the king-sized mattress. Then he started a timeline by using the blue tape to hang key documents on the wall under the stuffed moose head.

He stood back and sighed. "The place looks like a serial killer's lair. Or one of those guys who chases UFOs. All I'm missing is the crisscrossing red string."

Still, having all the pieces out and being able to sort and re-sort the documents made going through the crammed-full box less daunting. If George thought he'd cracked the case, Austin was prepared to believe him—he just had to follow the breadcrumbs.

Tossed on top of the items in the box, like an afterthought, had been a photo of a much-younger Greg and a man Austin assumed was Uncle George. With a round face, curly hair, and a big smile, George looked like the jovial sort who belonged in an apron behind the deli counter or perhaps over the stove in a family diner—not exactly the flinty-eyed, chiseled-chin hardboiled gumshoe.

Then again, looking harmless gets people to talk to you. People clam up if you look like you could dislocate their arms.

Austin had the training to handle a situation if it turned violent, but he'd always been grateful that his time on the police force had spared him that particular nightmare. He'd swung a few punches and earned good scores on the gun range, but he'd preferred to use his people skills and computer know-how to find what he needed rather than roughing up the bad guys.

He finished the pot of coffee and made another, absorbed in George's files. Thomas had been one of sixty-four patients who either disappeared from Havenwood or were "transferred without proper paperwork" between 1950 and 1980. Huffman wasn't the primary staff physician for all of them, but he would have had access even before he rose to oversee the adolescent department. It was clear from George's notes that Huffman had drawn the detective's attention.

"Holy shit," Austin muttered.

"In every case where patients supposedly transferred with insufficient paperwork, the receiving institution had no knowledge or record of their transfer," the notes read. *"Havenwood paperwork indicated the 'therapeutic relocation,' even including the names of real staff doctors at the other facilities, but neither*

documents nor patients ever reached the destination—and no one reported it or looked hard to account for the missing people."

Austin sat back and let that sink in. "They picked patients who didn't have family or whose families didn't care. So no one paid any attention."

Grandma Helen cared, but her parents hadn't. She thought Thomas died shortly after being taken away, which was what her parents told her to make her stop asking about him. The other families Austin identified were also cases of younger siblings looking for the truth long after the fact.

That level of betrayal and negligence on the part of the parents made Austin's blood boil. *All because the teenagers were different—abilities other people didn't understand or were frightened by. So many lives destroyed for nothing.*

Austin and Jamie had eaten all the pizza the night before, but he got the phone number off the box in the trash and ordered a meatball sub, salt and vinegar chips, and a Coke to be delivered, so he didn't lose momentum.

While he waited, Austin picked up one of the "witness testimony" folders. George had talked to Susan Lockwood, the same senior nurse, whose son had told Austin what he remembered about his mother's job at Havenwood. Susan had apparently unburdened herself directly to George.

Susan: *I didn't believe it at first, of course. That sort of thing only happened in movies. But then they brought Wally in—nice kid, probably about fourteen, skinny and defiant—and Doc Huffman started "examining" him. Only it wasn't a normal examination. He was poking and prodding the boy, trying to get a reaction, trying make him lash out. Hurting him on purpose.*

And then—this is the honest truth—a water pitcher lifted up off the counter all by itself and dumped over Huffman. Wally smirked like he was proud of himself. I wouldn't have believed it if I hadn't seen it myself.

George: *What happened then?*

Susan: *Huffman ordered Wally to be sedated. He had that poor boy drugged to the gills. He couldn't defend himself—could barely walk. About a month later, Huffman said a "transfer" came through to another hospital out West. It happened fast and after-hours. I had a couple of days off, and when I came back, Wally was gone, and no one knew or cared much about it.*

Austin ground his teeth over a situation that happened before he was born. George had documented all the particulars about Wally's case, including the lack of any patient files at the other hospital.

Susan gave a detailed account—her witness statement alone went on for more than a dozen pages. Wally hadn't been the only one who had raised her suspicions. Brian had been a fifteen-year-old with anger issues who freaked out the orderly when his body unexpectedly became temporarily more hairy and his facial features changed, only to reverse days later. He had "run away."

Austin put the file down and paced around the room, trying to work off his anger. He splashed cold water on his face, made and drank another cup of coffee, and texted Jamie.

Austin: *How's your morning?* At this rate, Austin knew he wouldn't win an award for poetry.

Jamie: *Quiet so far. I went through a couple more memory boxes but didn't find anything. And that word is still scratched on the wall. I didn't imagine it.*

Austin: *Don't forget to eat lunch.*

Jamie: *I won't. Go find the bad guys.*

Austin sighed and set his phone on the table. A knock at the door made him freeze, then move cautiously to check before opening the door for the delivery driver just enough to exchange cash for his sub.

He forced himself to read news headlines on his phone while he ate instead of thinking about the case. All too soon the food was gone and Austin returned to George's files. He settled onto the couch and picked up Susan's folder again.

George noted that Susan had raised concerns about the missing patients, only to be ignored and threatened with disciplinary measures.

Susan: *So a couple of us decided to do something about the problem. We couldn't save all of them. For one thing, we didn't have the same kind of access to all the patients. But one of the orderlies knew someone who could help us. They promised that if we could get patients out of the hospital, they could move them through "friendly hands" into Canada. So we did what we could.*

Austin stopped and re-read the passage. "Fuck. She started an Underground Railroad for paranormals. Go, Susan!"

Susan: *I asked why the orderly's contact couldn't just come and take the patients if they had their own "special abilities." He said that the hospital had wardings to keep them out and that the magic probably made the patients act worse, like a burr under a saddle.*

"No shit," Austin muttered. He thought about his visit to Havenwood the day before. While the experience hadn't been pleasant, he hadn't felt any compunction against entering—aside from common sense. His vision and Jamie's ghost whispering hadn't been affected. Then again, Huffman had died forty years ago. Austin didn't know squat about magic, but he guessed any "wardings" had lost potency over that length of time.

Austin's phone rang, and he glanced at it hopefully, but instead of Jamie's name, he saw Brent Lawson's. "Hey, Brent. What did you find?"

"Two of the names checked out—no criminal record, no

sketchy connections. I doubt three of the five people you asked me to look into could get a job anywhere near a respectable hospital these days," Brent replied. "They each had priors before Havenwood—petty theft, breaking and entering, that sort of thing. What's interesting is that those three left in 1980, and it didn't go well for them. Within a year, they were dead under questionable circumstances."

"Questionable?"

"One of them 'passed out' and drove his car into a lake. Another choked on his own puke when he was blackout drunk...but friends said he didn't drink. And the third overdosed on prescription meds that weren't prescribed for him."

"And no one found that unusual?"

"No one probably had a reason to connect them after they quit working for the hospital," Brent replied. "They didn't live in the same town. And they weren't the kind of people cops spend a lot of time wondering about."

"That's good info. Thank you." Austin hesitated, then figured Brent couldn't think he was any more bonkers than he probably did already. "Got a new question for you. If someone could put up wardings around a building to keep out people with certain talents, how long would those last?"

"You think someone put wardings around Havenwood?" Brent asked, sounding intrigued but skeptical.

Austin recapped what he'd learned so far from George's notes, including Susan's testimony.

"Fuck. You've really stepped in it, haven't you?" Brent replied. "Okay, quick primer. Magic is real, supernatural creatures exist. Magic is different but a little related to things like getting visions or seeing ghosts. Mostly, it's a talent people either have or don't have. But spells—and a warding is a type of spell—require energy to set in place, and they have to be renewed every so often. If not, they fade over time. So if your dicey doctor left four decades ago and no one bothered to refresh the wardings, I can't promise that they'd be gone entirely, but they'd probably be a lot weaker than they used to be."

"Probably?" Austin focused on the case and figured he'd have a private little freak-out about the whole "magic is real" thing later.

"It depends," Brent replied. "How strong was the one who cast the wardings? Are the spells tied to some sort of relic or talisman that acts like a 'battery' to store power? That would make them last longer. Like I said...it depends."

"How about Huffman? Did you find anything on him?" Austin had started to pace again, frustrated and antsy.

"Yeah. He was a real peach. Huffman was fired from his next position after Havenwood for 'inappropriate conduct,' which wasn't fully explained in the reports I found," Brent replied. "Then he went into solo practice and had ties to an iffy private rehab facility that got shut down for all kinds of violations—including patient escapes. A couple of his associates had ties to a known Huntsman. My bet is that he got paid to tip off the Huntsman about troubled teens who were just coming into their abilities, who then got kidnapped."

Austin swore under his breath as Brent continued. "That sort of thing is hard to prove, but while Huffman was in practice, there were half a dozen 'runaways' in that age bracket who were never found. Huffman died of a sudden heart attack—but that's easy to fake."

"You think he was murdered?"

"I wouldn't be surprised," Brent answered. "Maybe he was ready to retire, and he wasn't going to be useful anymore, but he knew too much. Or maybe he got greedy and decided to blackmail someone. Be careful, Austin. The type of people who get involved in this kind of thing play for keeps."

"Gotcha. Thank you. I'll let you know what happens," Austin promised.

Austin finished his Coke and poured another cup of coffee. He saw a new text from Jamie and smiled, glad for a distraction.

Jamie: *Where do you want to go for dinner tonight? I'll take care of dessert.* An emoji with a wicked grin accompanied the comment.

Austin: *You pick. I'm fine with anything as long as we're together.* Austin's thumb floated over the send button for a moment, realizing that his comment applied to more than just dinner. Deciding to walk on the wild side, he sent the message and hoped Jamie understood the full meaning.

Austin tossed the trash from his lunch and washed his hands so he didn't damage the old files. Then he made himself comfortable on the couch and picked up a folder marked "John Does."

The black and white photos of bones in a shallow grave stopped him cold.

George had stapled a typed note to the inside of the folder's cover.

"I made every effort to correlate the disappearance dates and descriptions of Havenwood patients with the discovery of unidentified remains across the US that had an estimated death date between 1950 and 1980. I found enough matches to suggest that some of the missing patients died far from Havenwood.

"Some of the bodies had been shot by a hunting rifle. They were found in unmarked graves on the private estates of three wealthy men who were known for their love of big game

hunting and their links to the occult. Those men eventually went to prison for tax fraud, embezzlement, and insider trading. Several other graves had remains that matched dental records of missing patients but did not show evidence of being shot.

"It is my considered opinion, based on witness testimony and the information gathered here, that patients who possessed certain special abilities were drugged and abducted from Havenwood and trafficked to buyers who either wanted to hunt them or forced them to use their talents for the gain of the abductors.

"Multiple witnesses claimed to see Dr. Huffman keep detailed research notes about illegal experimentation he did on the special patients, to determine the type and strength of their abilities. He may also have kept track of where certain patients were sent when they were taken away from Havenwood. Those files did not come to light when Huffman fell under later investigations. No one knows what became of them, but witnesses agree that Huffman documented everything and locked up his notes.

"Based on the testimony of witnesses and family members, I believe the patients possessed rare paranormal talents, including in some cases the ability to shift their form into something else. Some were psychics, and others could see ghosts. Their talents alarmed their families and led to them being committed, but I don't believe they were actually mentally ill.

"A great disservice was done to these young people. Although I believe the evidence here proves my theory, I know it will be inadmissible in court and laughed out of any law enforcement agency. Still, I believe it is important to bear witness to the wrongs done in the hope that such atrocities can be avoided in the future."

The document bore George's signature and a date.

Austin couldn't argue with George's conclusion that no matter how detailed his evidence, it couldn't be used in court. Still, seeing the information documented provided important validation. Austin couldn't help feeling both sad and vindicated.

He pulled out his phone.

Austin: *Found some interesting stuff Can't wait to show you after dinner. Did you pick a place to eat yet?* He sent the text, then picked up another file he hadn't read.

The new folder had more witness interviews, nurses, orderlies, janitors, housekeeping staff, groundskeepers—all the people who were in positions to see what was happening and notice patterns but had no power to intervene.

George had done his due diligence, and once Austin got used to the older man's handwriting, he started to pick up on the detective's voice and wry sense of humor. Austin thought about the burden George had carried in his heart for the missing patients all those years and perhaps guilt that he hadn't put the pieces together quickly enough to save some.

What about the ones that were spirited away to Canada?

Austin shuffled through the other folders, but he didn't find anything that indicated George tried to find the patients who had crossed the border. *Then again, why would he? Their families—or at least their parents—hadn't cared enough to notice they went missing. If they made it to Canada, in some sort of supernatural witness protection program, George probably didn't want to endanger them or the people who helped them by calling attention to the process or naming names.*

I wonder whether Thomas was lucky enough to go to Canada. I wish I could give Grandma Helen good news, even if she can't get in touch with him.

More to the point—what happened to Huffman's files? Did he take them with him? Were they lost or destroyed when the hospital was decommissioned? Or did he hide them somewhere on site?

On a hunch, Austin pulled up the photos of Havenwood's floor plans on his laptop, so the drawings were easier to read than on his phone. Zeroing in on Huffman's office was easy. Austin recognized the layout from the short time he and Jamie had spent there. There certainly hadn't been anything of value in the desk, cabinets, or filing drawers—they had made sure of that.

He was about to push the floor plans away when he realized something, and his eyes narrowed as he studied the drawings again.

I don't remember a storage room. There were bookshelves all along that wall. No door. We would have checked it out. There must be a hidden room behind those bookcases. Fuck. We need to go back to Havenwood.

This time, Brent Lawson picked up on the second ring. "Hi, Austin. Whatcha got?"

Austin summarized George's findings and described the documents in his box.

"Holy shit. The guy did a great job. But he's right. It would have never flown if he tried to press a case. What are you going to do with it?"

"I still haven't gone through everything yet. I want to see if he found anything about Thomas or the other family members on my list," Austin replied. "But I did want to pass along the names of the bigwigs who were behind at least some of the trafficking." He read off the names, spelling them for good measure.

"One of these I recognize right off the bat. Anything the Feds have on him is only half or less of what he's done. On the supernatural side of things, he's known for dark magic, relic theft, stolen artifacts, and a bunch of other stuff—all of it bad. I'll look up the others. That might put us onto their associates, which could help us at least find out what happened to more of the missing people."

Brent hesitated, and his voice softened. "I wouldn't get anyone's hopes up, Austin. Between the elapsed time and the type of people we're dealing with...I don't think there are any happy endings."

"Except for the lucky ones—who got to Canada." Austin sighed. "And on those, I agree with George's approach—leave well enough alone."

"Good. Because I was ready to argue you out of trying to look for them," Brent said.

"I'll let you know if we find Huffman's papers in that hidden room," Austin replied. "And think about what I should do with George's files. I'd like to pass them on to someone who can keep them safe and who knows about this stuff."

"I have a couple of ideas. I'll get back to you on that."

Austin ended the call, thinking that he'd have a lot to tell Jamie tonight and wishing that more of it was good news. Speaking of which...

He checked the time and then his text messages. He'd gotten absorbed in George's files and lost track. Two hours had passed without a response from Jamie. That seemed odd, especially on a day when Jamie didn't have any special events.

Memories of his warning visions sent a chill down Austin's spine as he dialed Jamie's number. *He probably just got busy, like I did. Or maybe something came up with his boss. I need to play this cool, or I'll look like some crazy possessive stalker boyfriend.*

Jamie's number rang, but no one picked up. Finally, the call went to voice mail. Austin stared at the phone like it was a snake about to bite.

Something's wrong. His certainty wasn't normal worry; it was the kind of hunch that had helped him close cases and kept him from getting killed.

Moving quickly, Austin gathered up the materials on the bed and put them back into the box, which he hid in the closet under his duffel, the best he could do on short notice. He didn't want to take the time to remove the items from the walls, but with the drapes shut and the *Do Not Disturb* hanger on the doorknob, no one should be around to see.

Fearing he'd already lost enough time, Austin grabbed his keys and headed to the Historical Association. The lights were on—nothing unusual since an hour remained before closing time.

The front door was unlocked, and the sign hadn't been turned. Austin looked through the glass and didn't see anyone inside. He felt hyper-aware of the weight of his Sig in the holster at his back. Austin really hoped that he didn't need his piece.

"Hello? Jamie?" he called out when he entered, already figuring that if Jamie popped out of the break room safe and sound, Austin would blame his overprotectiveness on another vision. *I don't mind being embarrassed as long as he's safe.*

His heart sped up when no one answered. Austin slowly moved into the space and pulled his gun, keeping it low in front of him to be out of sight of the windows. He didn't see any signs of a struggle, and no blood, thank God. Nothing looked damaged or missing. *Doesn't look like anyone ransacked the place.*

Austin remembered that Jamie talked about the room

upstairs where the "Through Their Eyes" boxes and other things were stored. Austin found the steps and headed up, with his gun raised and ready. Something crunched under his shoes, but he didn't see anything when he looked down.

The downstairs looked so thoroughly like a library that Austin had forgotten that it was a converted house. He ignored the small local author library and the meeting room, focusing on a large former bedroom filled with shelves that were lined with storage boxes.

Scratched into the plaster with deep gouges was the word "safe," the same word a ghost had written on the dirty window at Havenwood.

Austin stared at the word, and sudden comprehension hit him like a bucket of cold water. He remembered his vision of the nurse taking files from a green box and the clerk at the magic emporium being certain that the list of numbers on the note would meet Austin's "dire need."

What if it had nothing to do with us being safe? Huffman kept his files locked up in his secret room. Maybe he kept them in a safe.

He knew the truth of his guess as soon as it came to mind. *But where is Jamie? Because he's definitely not safe if he's not here.*

Austin moved into the room carefully, sweeping the area as his police training had taught him. Four rows back, he saw an overturned box, scattered papers, and a splotch of something dark on the wood floor. Grains of salt were everywhere.

Blood, Austin realized when he bent down. *And salt. Dammit. Whoever did this didn't want the ghosts to interfere. Salt dispels spirits. Fuck.*

All the evidence pointed to a struggle, with Jamie being

overpowered and injured. Anger flared, and Austin did his best to tamp it down.

I need to keep a clear head to find Jamie and get him back from the SOBs that took him.

Austin didn't know who was to blame for Jamie's disappearance, but the icy certainty in his gut told him where to look.

Those visions of Jamie being in danger—they're coming true, right now.

And it's up to me to save him.

10

JAMIE

Seven hours earlier.

Jamie hummed as he drove to work from Austin's motel. He left his bag and the rest of his stuff in Austin's room, happy that they were staying together. Their dinner date tonight gave him something to look forward to, and Jamie couldn't remember the last time his heart felt so light.

I want to keep him.

Most of the guys Jamie had dated didn't consider a relationship a priority if they could get regular sex. For a while, he'd gone along with that, mostly because he began to doubt anyone else wanted more. When the satisfaction gained from convenience no longer balanced out the hollow feeling it left behind, Jamie just kept to himself.

He hadn't realized how lonely he was until he met Austin.

I'm more sure of the way I feel about Austin after a short time together than I was about guys I dated for months. It's fantastic —and scary.

I think I love him.

Am I going too fast? What if he doesn't feel the same way?

The swoopy feeling in his stomach was a mix of excitement and fear. It reminded him of a vacation when he'd had Mimosas for breakfast and rocked a light buzz before he finished his omelet.

He remembered the way Austin touched him in the afterglow, gentle and almost reverent. The glint in his lover's eyes that shifted from lustful to possessive to affectionate. The way his voice could go from a sexy growl to caring reassurance.

I know he cares about me. But will he want to do the work to see if we can make this last?

Taking a gamble was risky, but Jamie wasn't willing to go back to the way things were before he met Austin without giving their relationship his best effort.

Jamie parked behind the Historical Association and walked to the coffee shop across the street, picking up a latte and a sandwich for lunch. He had just let himself inside the archive when his phone rang. Jamie couldn't help feeling a little disappointed to find out it was Simon Kincaide instead of Austin.

"Hi, Simon! What's up?"

"I figured I should check in and make sure you're okay. How's everything going?"

Jamie dropped his voice even though no one else was in the building. "We found some really interesting stuff. Your theory was right. Still haven't located Austin's great-uncle."

"I know you said Austin is a private investigator, but please be careful, Jamie," Simon warned. "I nearly got myself killed investigating a case on my own. Even people without special 'talents' can be very dangerous."

"I promise," Jamie replied, nearly whispering. He didn't want to risk being overheard filling Simon in on what had happened at Havenwood. "And I'll keep you posted."

Simon's call brought down Jamie's mellow mood. Once the lights were on and he'd started a fresh pot of coffee, Jamie felt some of the tension drain away.

Texting Austin cheered Jamie up.

I wish I could lock the door, but I can't. But I should be safe in a public place.

Jamie went through the morning checklist, hurrying any time he wasn't within view of the front windows. He booted up the computer, checked the fax machine, and made sure he retrieved any messages off the answering service. Some of that technology seemed as archaic as the rest of the museum, but Jamie was well aware that academics and limited budgets were sometimes resistant to change.

In between, he and Austin exchanged texts. Even though the texts weren't about anything monumental or even particularly romantic, the ongoing conversation made Jamie's heart warm.

His morning turned out to be busier than usual, although he still managed to exchange flirty texts with Austin. Quincey stopped by to pick up fliers for next week's community event, then stuck around to research something for one of his pet projects. A history teacher from the local high school dropped in to make sure everything was set up for her class's field trip later in the week, and Mrs. Gray from the Saranac Knitters Club popped in long enough to pin a notice about their upcoming meeting on the bulletin board inside the front door.

By the time Jamie finished with these interruptions and handled his email, his stomach growled, and a glance at the clock surprised him. *One o'clock already? That means I'm all the closer to dinnertime—with Austin.*

Jamie asked Quincey to keep an eye on the front door so he could eat a quick lunch in the break room. After that, time dragged. No one else came in, and Jamie plodded through a sequence of boring-but-necessary tasks, eager for the day to be over.

Mid-afternoon, Harold Winters, the librarian, waved hello through the window and came inside.

"Mr. Winters. How can I help you?" Given the mission overlap between the Historical Association and the library —and the school connections—Winters was a frequent drop-in. Jamie always gritted his teeth during the librarian's visits since the man's sour disposition got on his nerves.

"You've been wanting to talk about that 'Eyes' exhibit. I figured now's as good a time as any."

Jamie stared at the man in surprise. Winters had always seemed uninterested in the project when Jamie had approached him before. The memory box project had been set up long before Jamie came to town, and he vaguely remembered the exhibit being a joint venture with the library and several other community organizations.

"Sure," Jamie said, trying to cover his surprise and annoyance at needing to spend more time with Winters. "That would be great."

"How many boxes do we have?" Winters gave Jamie a sharp look like this was a test.

"Forty-five. But Richard only had a chance to put twenty into the system before he got sick. I've been entering them a few at a time as I can work it in around everything else."

Winters was friends with Jamie's boss, and he didn't want to leave any chance for information to get twisted with the telling. "It's not a formal part of my job, so I work on it when everything else is done," he added.

"I'd like to take a look at the boxes if you don't mind," Winters said.

Jamie glanced toward the door. "I should lock that since I'll be upstairs with you."

Quincey looked up from his place at one of the work tables. "I don't mind watching the door."

Reluctantly, Jamie agreed since he couldn't come up with a good reason to protest. Winters followed Jamie to the steps and trailed behind him as they climbed. He was glad he had pushed some boxes in front of the gouged word in the plaster since he didn't want to explain it to the librarian. His phone vibrated, letting him know he had a new text. He'd need to wait before replying to Austin, but hopefully Winters's visit wouldn't last long.

"We've had a great response to the program," Jamie said, tapping into his genuine enthusiasm for the Through Their Eyes effort. "I think when it's all put together, the materials will provide a really different view than what you get in most museums."

Winters wandered up and down among the shelving rows as Jamie talked, peering now and then at the boxes without pulling any out to look closely.

"Is there anything in particular you'd like to see?" Jamie asked. Winters was never his favorite person, but something about today was starting to creep him out. He had learned a long time ago to trust his gut, and right now his intuition told him he needed to get the hell out of the storage area.

Something crunched under Jamie's foot, surprising him since the cleaning team had been there just a few days ago. He bent down and pressed his fingertip against the floor, frowning as he recognized what had been spilled.

Why is there salt on the floor?

As Jamie straightened, he heard footsteps behind him.

Before he had time to speak, the barrel of a gun poked into his back, and he felt a sting in his neck.

"You've become inconvenient."

Jamie recognized the voice—Ed Thompson, one of the old men from the diner. Jamie's vision blurred, and his legs felt rubbery.

"Feeling it?" Ed asked with a sick smile, stepping around to where Jamie could see him. He had a gun in his right hand and held up a syringe in his left. "Army medic. You never forget some skills."

Jamie dropped onto his knees. *Quincey had to have seen Ed come in. He knows Winters was here. If I disappear...*

"Don't pin your hopes on Quincey," Ed said. "It's no accident he came over today. His job was to make sure we're not disturbed."

Jamie swayed, then fell flat, splitting his lip. His body refused to heed his commands, and his thoughts had grown fuzzy.

Ed zip-tied Jamie's wrists and ankles and stuffed a kerchief into his mouth. "Can't have you making noise."

They know about the ghosts. The salt kept them from interfering.

Even with the sedative slowing his mind, Jamie sensed the ghosts, agitated and angry. They knew what was happening and didn't like being forced away.

I didn't get to answer Austin's text. I'm not going to have a chance to say goodbye.

———

JAMIE REMAINED aware enough to be surprised Ed had the strength to lift him under his arms and drag him down the steps. Winters went first, spreading more salt on the steps and then down the back hallway to the rear door. Outside, Ed trundled Jamie into the back of an SUV and slammed the hatch. Moments later, they pulled away from the archive.

He drifted, not quite unconscious but too foggy to move or think clearly. When the SUV hit bumps, Jamie bounced across the cargo area, making the throbbing in his head even worse. The plastic ties bit into his skin, and his mouth felt dry and sore from the gag. Jamie knew he was in a lot of trouble.

The SUV rumbled to a stop with a lurch that banged Jamie's head against the seat support, and a thin line of blood trickled down his temples from the cut. Ed and Winters got out, but while Jamie could hear them talking, he couldn't make out their words. The hatch opened, and Ed reached in, grabbing Jamie by the ankles and yanking him to the end of the cargo area before roughly maneuvering him to his feet.

"C'mon. We've got a ways to go—and I'm not carrying you," Ed muttered.

Shouldn't have given me that shot. I can't feel my feet.

Ed and Winters each grabbed an arm and half-lifted, half-dragged Jamie across a lawn, tugging him through the high grass. They shoved him through the break in a chain-link fence, and the sharp edges of the steel ripped at Jamie's clothing. He shivered since they hadn't bothered to get him a coat.

Gonna kill me. Won't need one.

Even addled by the drug, Jamie recognized Havenwood. The gag muffled his protests, and he couldn't rally his body's cooperation to fight.

"Do we have to haul his ass up the steps?" Winters grumbled when they reached the main lobby.

"It's too open here," Ed countered. "We want his boyfriend to come to us somewhere we can keep control. There are too many entrances and too damn many windows here. Give me a hand."

Jamie bit down on the gag against the pain when his shins hit every marble step as he was hauled between two shorter men.

Austin will come looking when I don't show up for dinner. And if he finds me, they'll kill him too.

"Hope you brought a lot of salt," Winters said. "This place is haunted as hell."

Ed snorted. "These ghosts don't care. They never bothered us before. The ones at the archive mighta liked Jamie. Couldn't take that chance."

The ghosts are watching. They might not care or do anything about it, but they're waking up.

If he survived this, Jamie resolved to ask Simon Kincaide about the spirit medium side of his talent to see if he could learn how to better communicate with the dead.

Although I might be a ghost myself soon.

Other than reading books and watching some mostly useless YouTube videos, Jamie hadn't tried to control his ability to see ghosts. He hadn't figured he'd ever actually use it. Jamie had viewed his "ghost whispering" as interesting but useless. He knew better now.

Jamie's head felt clearer, although his body remained sluggish from the drugs. The gag bit into the corners of his mouth, and the sharp edges of the zip ties cut into his wrists and ankles.

Ghosts of Havenwood! These men helped Doc Huffman. He hurt you. Please, help me.

Only silence answered his plea. Jamie fought the urge to throw up, knowing he would probably choke on his own puke with the gag in his mouth. His stomach tightened, and despite the sedative, panic flickered.

They'll use me to lure Austin. Then they'll kill both of us. Simon and that private eye friend of Austin's might follow up, but it'll be too late. If the sheriff sides with Ed and Winters, no one will bother investigating.

Ed and Winters dropped Jamie when they reached Huffman's office, and Jamie managed to twist to take the brunt of the fall on his shoulder and hip instead of his face this time. He grunted from the pain, and Ed chuckled.

"You shouldn't have meddled in things that were none of your business."

Jamie glared at him and mustered enough spit and anger to get one word out past his gag. "Why?"

Winters looked at him, contempt clear in his expression. "Why did we grab you? To shut you and your nosy boyfriend up. Why did we help Huffman? He paid well—and the world was safer without those supernatural freaks in it. Why did Huffman do it? The money was good from the Huntsmen and their clients. But I think he figured if he could remove rabid dogs and make a buck or two, it was a win-win."

Rabid dogs. Supernatural freaks. Jamie realized that he'd shied away from embracing his talent in part because he didn't want to be seen like that—that a part of him had applied those names to himself. He'd viewed the people he should have been asking for help through that lens.

"Or do you mean why do we still care?" Winters said. "You two were making waves, asking too many questions. Sooner or later, someone might pay attention. We got along just fine for forty years until you started poking your noses into things that weren't your business. I don't plan to spend my golden years in the slammer."

"Some ran away." Jamie's tongue felt thick and parched, but he managed to get the words out around his gag.

Ed gave Jamie's hip a vicious kick. "Yeah, and they had help. Lost us a bunch of money. We thought we knew who was working against us, but they were careful. And we knew that if staff started to disappear, people might notice. Damn bleeding hearts. No one was going to miss a few rejects with some screws loose."

Jamie swung his bound legs and swept Ed's feet out from under him for that comment, sending the man crashing to the ground.

"You stinking little son of a bitch!" Ed scrambled to his feet and drew his gun, aiming at the center of Jamie's forehead.

Jamie caught his breath, and his eyes widened, sure he was going to die.

I never got to tell Austin that I love him.

"Put that down!" Winters's voice carried all the authority of a librarian addressing a noisy gaggle of preteens. "We need him alive—for now."

"Why you?" Jamie's parched throat made his voice a harsh croak.

"I worked at Havenwood right after I got out of the army as a medic," Ed said. "Huffman took good care of me."

"Havenwood did a lot of good work; pioneered new treatments. I won't let anyone damage its reputation or the town's," Winters replied.

Even if murder was involved.

JAMIE TRIED to figure how long it had been since his kidnapping and reckoned by the angle of the light that he'd been gone at least two hours. *Austin will know something's wrong when I don't show up for dinner. But can he put the pieces together to find me? And will he get himself killed trying?*

"Why didn't you call the out-of-town guy right away?" Ed sounded pissed. Winters took Jamie's cell phone from his pocket, holding it up and waggling it so Jamie would be sure to see.

"I wanted to get us settled and give him time to stew—if he's even noticed yet," Winter replied with a cruel smile. "And I wanted Jamie here to be awake for the party."

"Doncha need to crack his password?" Ed watched Winters curiously.

Winters shook his head. "Nope. He's going to give it to me." He fixed Jamie's gaze. "Now be a good boy and tell me, or Ed shoots you between the eyes right now, and we leave your body for the rats before we hunt your buddy down at the motel and kill him there."

If I tell them my password, they'll use my phone to lure Austin into a trap. If I don't, they'll kill me and still go after Austin—but he won't have the benefit of knowing there's danger. Fuck.

"J-A-M-E," he said, with a glare that promised trouble if he got loose.

Winters smirked at Ed. "See? That was easy." He checked recent calls, and found Austin's number already set up in Jamie's contact list, then turned the volume way up so Jamie could hear.

"Jamie?" Austin sounded breathless and worried.

"Nope. He took a little ride with us. He's alive—for now."

"Let him go." Austin's voice dropped to a dangerous growl.

"If you want him, you'll have to come get him," Winters said easily. "Huffman's office, Havenwood Hospital. Bring all your notes on the case. We'll make a trade—him for the notes."

"I'm not going anywhere until I talk to him."

Winters rolled his eyes and gestured toward Jamie. Ed sidled close enough to pull down Jamie's gag, keeping the gun trained on him at point-blank range.

"Austin." Jamie's voice was a hoarse whisper. His split lip began to bleed again, and his mouth was painfully dry.

"Jamie. Thank God."

Ed shoved the gag back in place, and any thoughts Jamie had about fighting ended when cold steel pressed to his forehead.

"Listen carefully," Winters said. "No one in town will believe you if you try to get help. The police and the sheriff are on our side. Hand off your notes, agree to stop nosing around, and you and Jamie can walk out of here. You've got thirty minutes." He ended the call.

Ed shot his accomplice a look dripping with condescension. "Anything can be photographed and backed up online. His notes don't mean squat."

Winters tossed Jamie's phone onto the dust-covered desk. "You're right. But whether he brings the notes or not, he's dead—and so is our nosy little historian."

Whatever Ed had injected him with had mostly worn off, and as his mind cleared, Jamie took stock of his situation. He'd watched a YouTube video about how to break out of zip ties after scoffing at a TV show scenario, only to discover the hero's escape was plausible. Unfortunately, Ed and Winters weren't leaving him alone, and the way he needed to swing his arms for momentum to break the ties wasn't something they'd overlook.

On the plus side, he'd found a thin piece of metal on the floor and hid it in his palm. If he got a chance to break his wrist ties, he could use the metal to pry up the locking tab on his ankle restraints. Jamie looked at the debris within reach and fixed the layout of the room in his mind. *Anything can be a weapon.* He took stock of what he might be able to throw, kick, or knock over. Jamie swore that he wasn't going down without a fight, and he sure as hell wasn't letting Ed and Winters hurt Austin.

Jamie wondered if the Havenwood ghosts cared more about revenge than Ed expected. Asking again for their help might be a long shot, but it was the best one he had at the moment.

Havenwood ghosts! The two men who kidnapped me used to work here. They helped Doctor Huffman hurt patients and sent them away into danger. I'm trying to stop them. Please, help me.

Nothing happened. Jamie had hoped for a sudden cold spot, an eerie breeze from nowhere, or disembodied footsteps in the hallway. When the ghosts didn't respond, he slumped, discouraged. He and Austin had come so far on the case, but now it looked like Ed and his buddies might win after all.

"What if he doesn't come?" Ed asked, looking out the window nervously. "Maybe he's not as keen on his boyfriend as we thought."

"He'll be here," Winters said. "And then we'll put the whole issue to rest, permanently."

Please, Jamie begged the ghosts. *They hurt you. Help us stop them.*

Ed took up a sentry post where he could see the front doors while Winters and Jamie waited inside Huffman's office. Jamie rehearsed the moves from the zip tie video in his mind, planning to risk trying to break free as soon as Ed and Winters were distracted.

"He's coming." Ed slipped back into the office. "And he's carrying a folder."

"Maybe this will be easier than we thought," Winters replied. "He might be dumb—or desperate—enough to do exactly what we asked." His contempt showed clearly in his tone.

Footsteps approached, then stopped. Jamie tensed, ready to make his move. *Please*, he pleaded with the ghosts again.

"I'm here," Austin's voice came from the hallway. "Show me Jamie."

"Show us what you brought," Ed countered.

"You saw me come in. You know I brought the file. I want to see Jamie." Austin's voice had a take-charge confidence that sent a thrill through Jamie.

"Come to the door. You can see him just fine from there," Winters said. Ed moved into position at the side of the doorway where he could drop Austin with a shot before the investigator ever saw the threat.

Now or never. Jamie lifted his bound wrists, then brought them down hard with his elbows out, and felt the ties snap.

Ed wheeled and fired at Jamie. Jamie hurled himself to one side, and the bullet barely missed his head. He grabbed a bookend from the floor and threw it in Ed's direction, figuring from the potent cursing that he'd hit something.

Austin swung into the doorway and returned fire, shattering the glass behind Winters as the librarian ducked behind the steel desk. Ed shot back, forcing Austin into the hallway. Jamie rolled, but the desk was the only cover, and any second now Ed would surely pick him off like a carnival midway target.

Jamie couldn't free his ankles, so he scooted back into the corner between the large bookshelf and the outside wall and tore his gag out of his mouth. Ed and Austin traded more shots, while Jamie kept an eye on Winters. Sure enough, the librarian emerged from under the desk with a gun of his own and trained it on Jamie.

Jamie had nowhere to hide.

"Austin—give yourself up or Jamie dies," Winters called out.

"Hold your fire!" Austin's answer was instantaneous. "Don't shoot him."

"Slide your gun to me," Ed ordered. Jamie heard the scrape of metal on tile as Austin complied. Winters kept his gun trained on Jamie. At this distance, even a crap shot couldn't miss.

"Put your hands on top of your head—and keep them there," Ed continued. A moment later, he escorted Austin into the room. Austin exchanged a worried glance with Jamie.

"We know you've been poking around, trying to find evidence about the disappearances," Ed said. "You hit everywhere in town that keeps records. Probably even got that pain-in-the-ass retired detective to cough up his notes. That's okay. Once we're done here, we'll take a little ride to your motel room and burn everything."

Fuck, Jamie thought, feeling his hope collapse. They had come so far, for nothing.

"Which one of you shot at us the last time we were here?" Austin asked, still defiant.

Ed grinned. "That was me. Been a deer hunter all my life. I trashed the duplex porch and keyed your car too. but you just wouldn't back off."

"Enough talking," Winters said, turning his attention to Austin. "Doc Huffman kept his 'special' records in a safe. I'm guessing a clever guy like you knows how to open it."

Something flashed across Austin's face, too quick to catch, but the confusion and panic in his eyes was genuine. "I don't know how to crack a safe."

The numbers from that weird shop. Are they a combination? Jamie forced himself not to look at Austin since he didn't want to give anything away in his expression. *I'd say what we have here counts as "dire need."*

Winters shrugged. "Then I guess we're done." He turned his gun back on Jamie. "If you can't help, he's no use to us as insurance."

Please. Jamie didn't know whether he was beseeching the ghosts or begging for divine intervention.

"Wait!" Austin paled. "Let's figure this out." He glanced toward the bookshelves on the wall by Jamie's corner. "There's a door behind there, right? That's where Huffman's records room was. I guess he got thrown out before he could take all his stuff."

"They wouldn't let him back in the building, and none of us could get near his office. After he left, the director could open everything except Huffman's safe," Ed replied. "Since they didn't want anyone messing with it, they hid the room and did their best to bury the scandal. After a while, everyone forgot about the other room. Then you started sticking your nose where it didn't belong. I'm too damned old to let you ruin what's left of my life. We want whatever is stashed in the safe."

"He's stalling, Eddie," Winters said. "He already said he can't open it." He turned his attention and the gun back to Jamie.

"No!" Austin took a half-step forward, then froze as Ed cleared his throat, gun trained at Austin's heart. "I said I couldn't *crack* a safe. But...I think I might have the combination."

Jamie stared at Austin, wishing he could read minds. *Whatever he's planning, I need to be ready, in case I can help.*

Jamie didn't want to die, and he sure as hell wasn't going to let Austin die if he could stop it. But he'd rather go down fighting than just sit still and wait for a bullet.

"Shove the bookshelf out of the way," Ed directed Austin, twitching the barrel of his gun in that general direction. "Let's see what you can do with the safe."

"If I open it, and I give you all my notes...then there's no reason to kill us. No one believed that other private detective. And without evidence, no one would believe us. So you'll let us go?"

"Sure," Ed replied. "We'll let you go."

Jamie knew Ed was lying. He was certain that Austin knew it too.

Empty of books and binders, the shelves weren't impossible to move. Austin shoved them just far enough to reveal a door. Shrouded in cobwebs and dingy with dust, the door didn't look like it had been opened for decades.

"It's locked," Austin said, giving the knob a try.

A gunshot nearly deafened Jamie. The door swung open, with a bullet hole through the lock. "Now it's not," Ed said with a smirk.

"Jesus, Eddie! Take it easy," Winters protested.

Ed flipped him off and looked at Jamie, who was hunched in the corner. His wrists were free, but the ties still bound his ankles. "You, stay out here. Winters'll keep an eye on you." He turned his attention to Austin. "Let's see what you can do with that safe."

"I found what might be the combination," Austin told Ed. "It's in my wallet. You want me to open the safe; I need that paper."

Ed jammed the muzzle of the gun between Austin's

shoulders. "I got no problem with you getting your wallet. Try anything else, and you'll have a big hole right through the middle."

Austin swallowed hard, and his gaze flicked to Jamie, who saw so much unspoken in his eyes. *I'm sorry I got you into this. I never meant to hurt you. I care about you.* Jamie wasn't psychic, but Austin got the message through just fine and he did his best to convey the same in return.

Austin reached slowly for his wallet, drew it from his pocket, and teased out a folded piece of paper. "I wasn't sure what this was, at first. Just a bunch of numbers. But I think it could be a combination."

"I hope for both your sakes that it is," Ed replied, cool and collected while keeping the gun pressed into Austin's back.

Ed shoved Austin into the next room, where Jamie had only a limited line of sight. Winters didn't move, remaining between the desk and the big window, his gun trained on Jamie.

Please, Jamie called to the Havenwood ghosts. He could tell they'd drawn closer, watching and listening. They were either choosing not to show themselves, or Jamie's ability wasn't strong enough to see them, but he could sense their presence.

More of them had gathered than on his previous visit with Austin. They were unhappy, and some were furious. The calmer ghosts from the upstairs were here—Jamie recognized the feel of them in his mind. So were the vengeful spirits from the basement, the ones that had been frightening at a distance and were downright terrifying this close.

They're going to kill us and destroy all the evidence of what Huffman did. Please, help us stop them. Don't let them shoot us.

Nothing stirred, and Jamie swallowed back his disappointment. Ed and Winters would make sure no one found their bodies. They'd be Havenwood's last disappearances, not that anyone in Saranac Lake would bother looking. Their families would never know what happened to them.

Jamie and Austin wouldn't get to find out if they could make their connection last and blossom.

Anger shot through Jamie like lightning, and his gaze darted around the room, looking for an advantage.

"Don't try any hero crap," the librarian told him. "I've got a good aim. I'll drop you before you can get to your feet."

Jamie forced himself to breathe. Through the hidden doorway, he saw Ed holding a flashlight in one hand and the gun in the other, while Austin knelt in front of a big, old-fashioned green iron safe.

"I told your boss that hiring someone from outside was a mistake, even temporarily. We should have kept the place closed and taken our time to get someone who understood. Someone who wouldn't make waves," Winters said. "I was right; he was wrong—but you're the ones who'll pay for that decision."

If anyone's going to do something, it's got to be me.

Any moment, Austin would get the safe open, and then they'd die. *Fuck that.*

Jamie pulled his bound feet beneath him and pushed off, diving toward the large bookshelves. He grabbed the back edge of the case and yanked as hard as he could, toppling the wooden shelving with a loud crash. Before the dust settled, he tucked and rolled as Winters fired and missed him. Tile chips flew from the bullet's impact.

Jamie hooked a foot behind a cast-off office chair and sent it skidding toward Winters, then rolled as fast as he could to be anywhere else. He knew that his distraction was limited—the office wasn't that big, and there was no cover except for the desk, where Winters still stood.

Winters fired again, and this time Jamie wasn't fast enough. The bullet sliced across his left bicep, and he let out a yelp of pain as blood soaked his sleeve. In the other room, Jamie heard the sounds of a scuffle, shouts, curses, and a single gunshot.

Oh, God. Austin!

Winters had Jamie in his sights, and this time he couldn't miss.

Please, Jamie called to the ghosts. *We're going to die.*

The temperature plummeted, and the glass frosted over, seconds before unseen hands lifted Winters and threw him through the large window. His screams cut off abruptly as he hit the driveway two floors below.

"Winters?" Ed shouted.

Even without a clear view, Jamie knew from the crashes and thumps that Austin and Ed were grappling for the gun. Austin was much younger and in good shape, but despite his age, Ed was wiry and desperate.

Jamie pulled out the flat piece of metal that he had palmed earlier and used it to pry the catch loose on the tie around his ankles.

Ed came barreling out, wild-eyed and bleeding from a split lip. "What did you do to Winters?" he demanded, staring at the broken window from the middle of the office. Austin stumbled to the doorway of the back room, bleeding from a gash on his temple.

"I didn't do anything. The ghosts did it," Jamie countered, trying to pull Ed's attention away from Austin. The temperature dropped again, and angry, muffled voices sounded from all around them as a wind from nowhere sent papers and trash swirling.

"Fuck this." Ed ran for the stairs. Jamie followed as far as the doorway, feeling the energy shift as the ghosts pursued his fleeing kidnapper.

Jamie saw Ed reach the top of the steps through the open doorway. Ed's back suddenly bowed as if pushed by a powerful force, and then he fell, tumbling down the marble steps head over heels.

For a second, Jamie glimpsed gray figures at the railing of the second-floor landing, looking down on Ed's corpse. Then the wind stirred again and carried them with it, leaving nothing but an empty corridor. Jamie ran to the railing and saw Ed's body splayed, twisted and bloody on the marble steps.

Thank you. Jamie couldn't tell if the ghosts were still listening, but he wanted them to know how grateful he was.

"Jamie!" Austin rushed across the office, looking a little steadier than before. He gathered Jamie into his arms and held him tight. Jamie hugged back with all his strength, reassuring himself that they were both alive.

"Are you okay?" Austin pushed Jamie back far enough to look him over, eyeing the cut on his forehead and the fresh blood soaking his sleeve.

Jamie nodded, trying to force words past his dry mouth and the thudding in his chest. "Yeah. I am now. Nothing that can't be fixed. How about you?"

Austin gingerly touched the gash on his temple. "I'll be fine. He got me with the safe door."

11

AUSTIN

"We've got to get out of here," Austin said, still driven by adrenaline. There'd be time to think and feel later when they were both safe. He ripped away Jamie's torn sleeve and bound up the wound on his arm as best he could, grateful the bullet hadn't done worse.

"I need to get my gun and grab the stuff out of the safe. Can you stand?"

Jamie nodded, looking like he was starting to zone out from shock. "My phone is on the desk. Winters took it."

"I'll get everything and be right back. Don't move." Austin darted into Huffman's office and found his gun, pulled the clip from his pocket and quickly reloaded it before grabbing Jamie's phone and going back to the safe. Lucky for him, Ed had brought a reusable grocery tote to haul away whatever they found, and Austin figured Ed wouldn't need it anymore. The safe held ledgers and note-books, as well as a sheaf of old letters, all of which Austin shoved into the bag to study later. He ripped off the bottom of his shirt and wiped down anywhere he might have left prints, then got down on the floor and retrieved Ed's gun that had slid underneath, wiping it clean as well.

If I ever see that elf-guy in the weird shop, I owe him a steak dinner. He said that strange bag picked out what I'd have "dire need" for. I'd say today was plenty "dire."

Austin didn't find any money in the safe. Huffman's "valuables" were his contacts and research notes, as well as ledgers of names, the suspected abilities of the patients he betrayed, the names of buyers, and the prices paid, all of which made Austin's stomach turn.

Austin found Jamie leaning against the wall, pale and shaking.

"Come on," Austin said as he hung the tote on one shoulder and got the other under Jamie's good arm.

"Ed's down there." Jamie pointed toward the grand staircase, looking like he might be sick.

"It's too risky to try to find another exit," Austin replied apologetically. "We could get trapped, and we need to be gone from here. Focus on my feet, and when we get to him I'll guide you past with your eyes shut."

We're going out the back door, so at least we won't have to navigate around what's left of Winters too.

"Hospital?" Jamie asked.

"Not unless you want to explain a bullet wound," Austin said through gritted teeth as they started to navigate the steps. Jamie wasn't little or light, and Austin couldn't afford to slip on the marble stairs. "I've got butterfly bandages and a pro-level first-aid kit in the SUV. I promise I'll fix you up as soon as we're away from here. But I don't want to explain the two dead guys to the crooked cops."

Austin navigated around the blood on the white stairs, blocking Jamie's view of the worst of it. "Shut your eyes," he murmured when they neared Ed's body, and Jamie turned his face into Austin's neck as they maneuvered past.

"It's okay now," Austin said once they were out of sight. "How are you holding up?"

"Lightheaded," Jamie replied. "Cold. I want to throw up."

"That's shock kicking in," Austin told him. "You kept it together so well back there. So damn brave. You and those ghosts are the reason we both got out alive. Thanks for saving our asses."

"Ed was gonna shoot you. Couldn't let that happen." Jamie's words slurred, a mix of pain, adrenaline crash, and shock, Austin figured. Maybe a little hypothermia from the way Jamie was shaking.

"Are you hurt anywhere besides your shoulder?" he asked, concerned that Jamie had wounds he couldn't see.

"Hit my head in the back of the car. Fell a couple of times—probably bruised. Nothing big."

Austin let out his breath in relief. "Good." He was quiet for a few minutes as they left Havenwood behind them and started through the tall grass toward where Austin left his 4Runner.

"You scared the shit out of me," he admitted, tightening his grip around Jamie's waist. "I knew something was wrong when you didn't answer my texts. So I went to the archive and found blood up in the stacks—and got another vision. Then Winters called on your phone—"

"Quincey was in on it." Jamie's ragged voice reminded Austin that his boyfriend had spent hours gagged. Austin took a deep breath to cool his rage and reminded himself that the two men responsible were already dead.

"You can tell me later," Austin soothed. "Save your voice. I've got water in the car—that'll help."

Jamie collapsed into the front seat. Austin grabbed a

blanket from the back and tucked it around him, pressing part of it against his wounded shoulder.

"Keep some pressure on this, Jamie," he said. "Just for a while."

Then Austin started the engine and turned on the heat. He twisted the top off a bottle of water and held it so Jamie could drink. Austin drove them away from Havenwood, not stopping until he spotted an abandoned grocery store with a service road behind it. He parked where they were hidden from view but could still make a quick getaway if needed and patted Jamie's good shoulder.

"Hang tight for a minute while I get the kit." He went to the back hatch and returned with a larger-than-usual first aid box.

"Let me see your arm," Austin said, removing the cloth he had wrapped as a makeshift bandage. He helped Jamie out of his ruined button-down and pushed back the stained T-shirt beneath. The bullet had sliced across the meat of Jamie's arm below the shoulder leaving a painful gash.

It could have been so much worse, Austin thought. *Missed the bone in his arm and his shoulder, didn't hit an artery.* He'd had enough first aid training and field experience as a cop to know what could go wrong.

"Probably hurts like hell, but it's not deep enough for me to risk stitching it," Austin said. "The strips should close it up so it heals well. Can't promise you won't have a scar."

"Thanks," Jamie mumbled, looking like he might pass out.

"Lean against the window," Austin said. "That way, if you faint, you'll stay upright. Just don't puke."

"I'll try not to," Jamie said, shifting position.

Austin ignored how his hands shook when he cleaned the wound, and he didn't miss Jamie's wince at the pain.

"Almost done," he said, being as gentle as possible. "I've got Advil for now—and some stronger stuff for later."

"I knew you'd come," Jamie said in a raw voice just above a whisper.

Austin had never felt panic like when he realized Jamie had been kidnapped. He'd been part of hostage stand-offs enough times as a cop to know they usually didn't end well. Any qualms he'd had over what he felt for Jamie and what he wanted from their relationship had been scoured away, leaving only certainty.

They could work out the details later. Right now, he needed Jamie clear-headed for some tough decisions.

"I'm so sorry I got you into this," Austin said as he placed the butterfly bandages and wrapped Jamie's upper arm with gauze. "This is all my fault."

Jamie laid a finger across Austin's lips, then shook his head. "No," he whispered.

Austin knew it wasn't fair to argue when Jamie couldn't hold up his end of the conversation. That didn't make his guilt any less. He put the kit away, handed Jamie some Advil to swallow with the water, and got back into the 4Runner.

"It's not safe for you to stay in Saranac Lake," Austin broached the hard truth. "If Quincey goes to the cops and they find Ed and Winters, it won't look good, and there's no way to explain the ghosts. I'm so sorry...I've cost you your job."

Jamie glared at him. "Crummy job. What now?" The water had helped, but his voice still sounded scratchy and painful.

"Let's go get your stuff from the duplex and then clean out my motel room—and hole up somewhere to catch our breath," Austin said. "We'll figure it out from there."

If they got out of the local sheriff's jurisdiction, they'd be harder to arrest. Austin mentally cataloged the favors he could call in if needed. Meanwhile, he needed to protect Jamie. Since he figured it was his fault Jamie had to quit his job, Austin had no qualms about covering their costs while Jamie planned his next move.

The true test of a relationship is going on the run together from the cops.

"Okay." Jamie looked like he'd been in a bar fight and lost, but Austin recognized the stubborn set to his jaw and the glint in his eyes—despite the pain—that clearly showed that he'd made up his mind.

"Kinda like Butch and Sundance. Or Benny and Clyde."

That got an amused snort out of Jamie.

Austin had to hope that Ed and Winters weren't professional enough to have someone watching either the duplex or the motel. He had no idea how long it would take for Quincey to raise an alarm or at least send the crooked sheriff out to Havenwood. A lack of hard evidence wouldn't stop the local police from arresting them and holding them overnight—long enough for "accidents" to happen. Given that this crowd had already shown themselves willing to kill to bury old secrets, Austin had no intention of letting either of them be taken into custody.

He backed into the driveway next to Jamie's place, leaving the nose of his SUV sticking out and even with the parked cars on either side so no one could easily park him in. "Come on—I'll help you pack."

"Won't take long. Only been here a month." Jamie got out of the car on his own and headed for the door, with Austin trailing behind protectively.

"Throw your clothes into a suitcase and everything else into laundry baskets," Austin instructed. "Leave stuff like food and toiletries—that can be replaced."

Working together, they were done in half an hour. Jamie had a box of books he hadn't unpacked and some DVDs and more books in the living room, along with a few favorite mugs, the coffee maker, and a couple of good pans from the kitchen. Austin packed the housewares and sundries after Jamie pointed out what was his, as well as snacks for the road.

Jamie insisted he was fine to grab clothing, shoes, boots, and personal items from the bedroom, as well as the small TV he had brought with him, and reminded Austin that he had already taken his laptop, e-reader, and gaming console when they stopped earlier for clothing. All the while, Austin kept glancing nervously out the window, watching for a cruiser with flashing lights.

"Place came with the job, so I don't have to break a lease," Jamie said as he left the key on the counter on their way out. "I guess that's a plus." He sounded better, but Austin knew that once the Advil wore off, Jamie was likely to crash hard. At least now he had a coat, so Austin didn't need to worry about frostbite. "Ed said he was the one who trashed the porch. Fucking asshole."

"Do you have anything you need at the archive?"

Jamie shook his head. "Just my car. I left my jacket on the front seat this morning, but my heavy coat is here with my boots. I knew I wasn't going to stay, so I didn't take in anything personal. I've been applying for other jobs."

Austin took it as a good sign that Jamie was speaking in longer sentences. "It won't take me long at the motel," he replied. "I figured I'd only be here a week or so."

Jamie's face fell at that comment, and Austin realized how it sounded. "Didn't realize I was going to fall in love working the case," he added and saw Jamie's eyes spark. "We haven't known each other long, and now your whole life is upended, but thinking that I might not be in time to save you made some things clear in my mind. Like how I feel—and what I want."

Despite his injuries, Jamie's smile was big and genuine. "Same here."

That warmed Austin, even though they weren't out of danger yet.

"But first, we need to get the hell out of Dodge," Austin added.

He only had one room to worry about back at the motel and a few sundries in the bathroom, some groceries that would keep in the car, plus his notes and George's box. They were out in minutes. Austin left his room key on the nightstand. He thought about leaving a note for Greg, but figured he could call later—if the local grapevine hadn't already given the motel owner enough to piece the truth together.

"My car?" Jamie asked.

"I don't think you should drive right now," Austin replied, taking in how shaky Jamie still looked. He reached over to take Jamie's hand. "Let's get settled, and I'll figure out how to send someone to get it."

———

AUSTIN HEADED SOUTH without any destination in mind other than to put as much distance between them and Saranac Lake as possible. They had been on the road for almost an hour, and he knew they needed to find a place for the night soon. He felt his adrenaline crash, revealing every sore muscle and a level of exhaustion that came from surviving a near-death experience. Jamie looked like he was fading fast.

Jamie's phone rang, and he checked the ID, relaxing as

he recognized the name. "Simon Kincaide—he's a friend, and he knows about ghosts. He's been helping me."

He put the call on speaker. "Hi, Simon." His voice was still lower and raspier than usual.

"Jamie—are you okay? I had a vision—"

Jamie managed a hoarse chuckle. "We're alive. Had to leave fast. I'm going to let Austin do the talking now."

"Hi, Simon," Austin said. "Thanks for helping Jamie. You don't happen to know a good place for us to lie low in the Adirondacks, do you?"

"Brent Lawson speaks well of you," Simon replied, and Austin's eyebrows rose. "He called me for advice on the Havenwood problem. You can fill us both in later. But as far as finding a bolt hole, Fox Hollow shouldn't be too far away. It's a special town with good people. You'll be safe there, and they can help."

"Thanks," Austin said. "Once Jamie's voice is better, we'll catch up with you and Brent."

"Take it easy and trust your gut," Simon told him. "After Brent called me, I got in touch with a few friends in Fox Hollow. They have some information you need to wrap up your case. Isabel will be in touch." He ended the call, and Austin finally felt like things might work out.

"Look." Jamie pointed to a sign that indicated Fox Hollow was coming up.

Austin didn't understand why he felt a sense of calm as soon as they rolled into town, but some of the tension that had tightened his chest eased.

"I think one of the jobs I applied to is in this town," Jamie said, still sounding like it hurt to talk.

"Stick with charades and interpretive dance until your voice gets better," Austin joked. "You don't want to damage your throat."

Jamie rolled his eyes, making his point eloquently without needing words.

Austin pulled into the Lucky Clover. The sign said *Motel/Campground/Cabins/Pizza*. "Wait here," he said and went into the office. It didn't take long to get them set up.

"I rented a cabin," he told Jamie when he returned. "We can stay on indefinitely. They seem pretty used to people sticking around for the season."

"Can't afford it," Jamie protested.

Austin took his hand again. "I can." Jamie shook his head, and Austin squeezed his hand. "Please, let me do this. I don't need to go back to Albany for a while, and I can work from anywhere. You'll have time to recover, and we'll have a chance to get to know each other without being shot at. We could both use the vacation."

Jamie looked like he was going to be stubborn about it, then relented with a nod and threaded his fingers with Austin's.

The cabin was even nicer than Austin expected. He'd rented one of the bigger "family-sized" units figuring that he and Jamie might need the elbow room. It had a full kitchen, a cozy living/dining area, a full bathroom, two bedrooms, a loft, and a stone fireplace. They'd never even gotten a chance to light the fireplace in his room back in Saranac Lake. Austin hoped they'd only be using one bedroom for sleeping, which left the other for an office. The exposed logs and pine paneling had a retro vibe, but the cabin had obviously been well-maintained, and the mission-style furnishings looked comfortable.

"Not too shabby," he said as he led Jamie inside, insisting on carrying both their bags.

"Nice," Jamie agreed. "And no moose head."

Austin dropped their bags in the larger bedroom and

went to check out the kitchen. "The man at the front desk said they keep the units stocked with basics, and I filled out a checklist for groceries. He'll just charge it to my card and deliver everything here. Oh, and I ordered pizza. Didn't figure we wanted to go out tonight or try to cook."

"Awesome," Jamie said, but he couldn't hide the pain and exhaustion in every line of his body.

"You okay with sharing a bedroom?" Austin asked, even though they'd been sleeping together the last few nights. He didn't want to assume.

Jamie nodded. "Please."

"Why don't you lie down, and I'll get us settled," Austin said. "The pizza should be here in about half an hour, and you should eat before I give you the 'good' pain meds."

Jamie practically melted, stretching out on the couch that was long enough to accommodate his full length. Austin ruffled his hair affectionately as he passed him on the way to the bedroom. He set their bags to the side, checked to make sure the bed was freshly made and set out towels and their shaving kits in the bathroom. Austin silently thanked Simon for his recommendation.

This cabin will do just fine while we get our feet under us.

A knock at the door made him freeze in alarm until he remembered the pizza. Jamie roused on the couch. But when Austin checked through the peephole he saw an elderly woman, not the delivery driver.

He drew his gun but kept it behind him as he opened the door.

"I'm Isabel," she said as if that explained everything. Despite barely coming up to Austin's collarbone, Isabel carried herself with self-assurance and radiated a confidence and power that his psychic ability recognized even if his brain still struggled to catch up.

"Simon Kincaide told you I'd come." She pushed past him, not waiting for an invitation. "Put that gun away. I'm a witch. If I wanted to hurt you, I'd have done it already."

Jamie had pulled himself up to a sitting position and tensed at the intrusion.

"A witch?" Austin echoed, feeling like he'd missed something.

"Try to keep up," she snarked. "You and Simon aren't the only ones who get 'glimpses.' I've been in Fox Hollow for a long time. Long enough to remember your great uncle Thomas—and the others."

Isabel seated herself at the table like she owned the place. "When we realized what Huffman was doing at Havenwood, we made connections with some folks on the inside who didn't like what they saw. We couldn't save every-one, but we got dozens of patients out of that hellhole. Gave them new identities and passed them through friendly hands to set up new lives in Canada. Only bad part was, they could never contact their families again."

She grimaced. "For most of them, that wasn't a big deal since their families sent them away. Your great-uncle was one of those people. He could see visions like you do—in case you wondered."

"He made it to Canada?" Austin felt relieved, although it unnerved him that Isabel seemed to know so much about him, things Simon couldn't have shared since Austin had never met or even talked to the man. "Is he still alive?"

Isabel shook her head. "Sorry, no. I checked once I real-ized why you were investigating. I'm going to ask you to be... discreet...in sharing information. Some of the runaways are still alive, and the people who helped them could get in trouble for their efforts."

"I have to let Grandma Helen know."

"Handle it the way you think best, but remember there's more than your great-uncle's story at stake," Isabel replied.

"I will," Austin said, feeling like he'd stepped into the Twilight Zone. He'd spent his whole life hiding his psychic abilities. Having Simon and Isabel talk about those talents so openly made him wonder just how "special" a place Fox Hollow really was.

Isabel turned to Jamie. "If you need a doctor, our hospital is used to handling unusual circumstances. You'll be protected." A crafty smile touched her lips. "And you should check your email."

Jamie frowned and immediately reached for his phone. "Holy crap," he said with a nervous glance at Isabel. He looked up at Austin. "That job I applied for last week in Fox Hollow? They made me an offer," he said incredulously. "High school history teacher...focus on Victorian studies." He shook his head. "That kind of turnaround is unheard of. It usually takes months, even when everything goes right."

"Works a little different in a town full of psychics, mediums, witches, and shifters," Isabel said with a smirk.

Austin's world tilted on its axis, and he saw Jamie's eyes go wide. "What did you say?"

Isabel smiled and waved her hand dismissively. "Don't worry—you'll get used to it."

She stood. "You can find me through the Fox Institute if you have questions. I should go. Your pizza is coming. Oh, and one more thing, your keys?" She looked right at Jamie.

Jamie looked at her in confusion but pulled out his keys and handed them over.

"Are you psychic? And why do you need Jamie's keys?" Austin asked.

She gave him a withering look. "No. I can smell the garlic from here—it'll probably give me heartburn for the rest of the night. But we do have several psychics in town, and if we're going to retrieve his car, it goes much easier with the keys. You kids have fun; I have some clean-up to do," she added with a knowing look over her shoulder before she was out the door and gone.

"Did that really happen?" Jamie asked.

"I think so?" Austin felt a bit adrift as well. "But you heard your friend Simon say we could trust them."

The next knock *was* the pizza and the grocery delivery. "We shouldn't have to go anywhere for several days," Austin said to Jamie after he tipped the man and carried everything to the kitchen. "After that, we can explore. Once you're feeling better."

"You're going to stay?" Jamie sounded worn and worried.

Austin cupped Jamie's face with his hand and leaned in for a kiss. "Yes. I can take a couple of weeks before I need to go check on things in Albany. And I'll be back as soon as I can after that. Even if I have to commute now and again for cases, it's only a couple of hours. Plus you've already got a job, so it won't take long for you to get settled in."

"I think some food, those pills you mentioned, and a good night's sleep should help," Jamie replied. He winked. "Hot sex wouldn't hurt."

"Hot sex and pain meds don't tend to go together," Austin cautioned. "Cuddle now—set the world on fire in the morning?"

Jamie gave a rueful smile. "Probably a good idea. I'm pretty sure the day's catching up to me."

They wolfed down the pizza straight out of the box, but Austin put the beer he'd ordered in the fridge for later, figuring it wouldn't mix with medication. Once he stashed the perishable groceries in the refrigerator and found shelves for the rest, Austin slowed down enough to feel the day come crashing down on him.

Tomorrow they could check out the DVD collection, the Wi-Fi, and the satellite TV reception. Austin wasn't sure he could stay awake long enough to brush his teeth, and Jamie looked ready to collapse.

"Come on," Austin said. "Let's get a quick shower to clean up. It'll help us sleep."

"I'm having all kinds of naughty ideas I don't think my body can follow through on right now," Jamie admitted.

"Hold onto those ideas for tomorrow," Austin said. "Sex is better when we're awake for it."

Jamie fell asleep almost immediately after the shower, snuggled up against Austin in the king-size bed. Both of them seemed to need the contact even more than usual, reassurance that they were alive after the day's close call. Austin figured the pain meds would ensure Jamie got deep sleep without nightmares.

He worried that his racing thoughts would keep him awake, but exhaustion triumphed over anxiety. Austin didn't wake until daylight peeked through the curtains, and a warm, wet mouth started sucking his cock.

"Good morning to you too," he said. Austin suspected that Jamie had a thing for morning wood, something he was more than willing to indulge.

Jamie pulled off with an almost pornographic *pop* and looked at Austin. He had spit-slick, plump lips and a look of pure naked lust in his eyes.

"I want you to fuck me." His growl went right to Austin's already aching cock. "I want to feel you inside me and celebrate being alive." He grinned. "I woke up a little while ago and went ahead and opened myself up, in case you said yes."

Austin wondered if he should pinch himself to make certain he wasn't dreaming. "Yes. *Si. Oui. Da. Ja.* I don't know any other languages." He reached down to tangle a hand in Jamie's hair and loved the way Jamie leaned into his touch.

"That's what I was hoping you'd say," Jamie replied, reaching under the covers to pull out a foil condom packet and lube. He leaned down to swirl his tongue over the head of Austin's cock again, then sat back on his haunches as he peeled the packet open. Austin raised his gaze to get a good look at Jamie's cock, which was just as scrumptious as he'd imagined.

"I'm negative, just so you know," he said as he carefully rolled the condom over Austin's leaking dick and slicked him up.

"So am I. It's been a while," Austin confessed. "Maybe we can go get a new test done together. I'd like to feel you without anything in between. I know we haven't talked about it, but I'm a one-man sort of guy. You don't have to worry about that."

Jamie smiled. "Good. Because I don't share."

"How do you want to do this so we don't hurt your arm?" Austin could come up with several options, all of them hot.

"I'd like to ride you," Jamie replied, managing to look shy and sexy all at once.

"Oh God, yes!"

Jamie shifted to straddle Austin's hips, reached behind to pull his cheeks apart, and then sank down slowly onto Austin's rock-hard cock. He hadn't been kidding about prepping himself because he took Austin's full, thick length without stopping, all the way to the root. Then he leaned back, making sure Austin had a good view of his cock sinking into Jamie's tight, slick heat.

Austin managed a groan, and Jamie's smile widened. "Like that?"

Austin nodded, not quite able to form words just yet. He brought his hands up to rest on Jamie's hips, needing to touch but letting Jamie take the lead. Jamie stayed still for a moment, eyes narrowed in pleasure. Austin had the presence of mind to grab the lube and slick his palm, closing one hand around Jamie's cock and stroking from balls to head with a firm grip.

"Might not set any stamina records this time," Jamie said, sounding breathy. "You're even better than I imagined."

"You imagined me?" Austin shouldn't have been surprised since he'd been jerking off to thoughts of Jamie since they met. He liked knowing that Jamie wanted him from the start as well.

"Oh, yeah," Jamie replied, starting a slow, shallow rise and fall that took Austin's breath away. "I have plenty of ideas. It'll take us a long while to work through them all." His smile turned lusty again. "Oh, and I love switching if you're up for it."

"I'm all for it," Austin managed as his hand set a lazy rhythm up and down Jamie's elegant cock.

Jamie swiveled his hips, and Austin saw stars. "You like that?"

"Uh-huh."

Jamie ran his hand up Austin's chest, exploring the expanse of skin, stopping to tweak his nipples.

"I want to explore all of you," Jamie murmured. "Taste you everywhere. Spend all afternoon edging you until you can't wait any longer. See how many times I can get you to come and lick you clean each time." He dragged his tongue across his lips, holding Austin's gaze.

Austin had never been partial to dirty talk in bed, but

Jamie seemed determined to press all his buttons and discovered a few Austin didn't know he had.

Jamie lifted up, nearly off of Austin's cock, and came down hard, then did it again and again, setting a demanding rhythm. Austin kept one hand wrapped around Jamie's dripping cock, while he slid the other up his side, across his chest, and down those deliciously flexing thighs.

He didn't know where to look, so his eyes darted from Jamie's blissed-out expression to the sinuous movement of his narrow hips, down to where his cock slipped in and out of Jamie's body. Austin moved his hand around to cup Jamie's ass and gave a squeeze.

"So close," Jamie groaned, arching backward, head back, eyes closed, looking to Austin like a debauched angel. He shifted, and Austin could see Jamie's body shudder as the new angle probably hit his sweet spot just right.

Jamie came down hard and fast, sheathing Austin to the hilt, and that was it. Austin bucked up, holding Jamie's hip tightly enough he might leave fingerprints as his climax thundered through him, and he shouted Jamie's name. He managed to stroke Jamie once, twice, and then Jamie spilled over Austin's fist, painting his chest with streaks of come that nearly reached his chin.

Jamie collapsed onto Austin, still joined, and Austin wrapped his arms around his lover, mindful of his sore shoulder.

"You are so beautiful," Austin murmured against Jamie's temple and kissed him gently. "I love you. And not just because you're amazing in bed...although you are."

"Wanted to impress you with my skills so you'd keep me," Jamie replied, sounding sated and dazed.

Austin let his hands roam over Jamie's back, appreciating the lean muscles and looking forward to ogling the taut ass he'd barely glimpsed once they got into the shower. "Already planning on keeping you, if you'll have me."

"Um...I wasn't going to let you go without a fight," Jamie replied, landing sleepy kisses across Austin's chest. "And unless we go clean up, we could end up stuck this way."

Austin felt the pool of cooling come between them and knew the risk was real. "I think the shower's big enough for both of us, although acrobatic sex in there is likely to break us or the enclosure."

Jamie shifted, and Austin slipped out. He felt the absence immediately and pulled Jamie up for a slow, lingering kiss. "That's okay. We have a whole cabin to break in."

Jamie kissed him back. Austin remembered how he'd answered the elf-clerk's question about what he wanted most. He smiled, realizing that he'd found a haven of his own, right here in Jamie's arms.

EPILOGUE

Six months later
JAMIE

"Welcome home." Jamie stretched up to kiss Austin and pulled him in tight for a hug. Grinding his erection against Austin's thigh served to remind his partner just how *hard* it had been for Jamie while Austin had been away in Albany.

"Missed you," Austin murmured, returning the kiss with passion, bucking his hips against Jamie to confirm that their separation had been difficult for him as well. "But the sale went through without a hitch. Selling the house was the last of Grandma Helen's estate to settle. One less reason for me to need to go back to Albany."

Jamie gave Austin another squeeze, knowing that while selling the house in Albany was a relief, his partner also grieved an ending.

"You gave her peace before she passed," Jamie reassured him. "She got closure about Thomas, and the best news possible, that he'd lived out his life happy and safe in Canada."

Austin shrugged out of his jacket and hung it over the tall handle of his roller bag. "Mom and I think that finding out for sure was what Helen needed to let go. It turned out that she was sicker than we knew, and she had asked her doctor not to tell us. Once she checked off the last thing on her to-do list—Thomas—she was ready."

"That's a huge gift you were able to give her," Jamie told him, taking the jacket and hanging it on a peg near the door. "And to all the families who finally got answers." He came back and took Austin by the hand, leading him into the living room.

"Are you hungry? Do you need something to drink?" Jamie asked as they settled onto the couch. "And once you get your bag put away, you need to see how good the new fence looks in the backyard. This place is starting to feel like home."

Austin took Jamie's right hand, letting his thumb gently twist the gold ring on Jamie's finger, the one that matched the ring on his own hand. "Anywhere we're together feels like home," Austin told him and leaned in for another kiss, sweet and lingering.

Within a month of landing in Fox Hollow after they'd left Saranac Lake, Jamie had settled into his new teaching job, and he and Austin had started looking for a house together. Grandma Helen had accepted Austin's somewhat-edited story about Thomas's escape with grace. Then she had surprised Austin by giving him and Jamie her blessing.

She died two days later.

"Think you'll miss Albany?" Jamie asked, relishing having Austin home.

He shook his head. "Not really. I mean, I'll go back to see Mom. But I was ready to move on—I just hadn't known it yet."

They'd found this cabin three months ago and closed on it quickly. Jamie had handled most of the logistics since Austin needed to manage getting Grandma Helen's house ready to sell and moving his belongings to Fox Hollow. That had been a lot of weight on Jamie's shoulders to get the cabin the way they wanted it, along with settling into a new job, but he felt like everything was finally coming together.

One month after they bought the cabin, Austin proposed, offering matching gold rings reforged from the ones that had belonged to Grandma Helen and Grandpa Stewart. Jamie had said yes before Austin had finished asking.

Now that Austin was in Fox Hollow to stay, Jamie knew they'd get around to setting a date. He already had ideas about where and when, but that conversation could wait until Austin settled in.

"Everything going okay at the high school?" Austin stretched out his legs and pulled Jamie close.

"Yeah. Real good," Jamie replied. "In fact, I wanted to wait until you got home to tell you the news. Russ Jeffries over at the Fox Institute asked me to help with a research project they're doing on the town's *real* history—shifters, psychics, and Spiritualists included. They have a supernatural historian and a photographer already on deck. I'd be part of the team. It's a perfect fit for my focus on the Victorian era."

Austin beamed and kissed Jamie on the cheek. "That's fantastic. Congratulations."

Jamie nearly bounced with energy. "Thanks. I'm excited about it. And I know it'll help me get to know more people here." He leaned against Austin. "Now that you're here for good, you can get into your new project too."

"Everything's been such a whirlwind, I haven't had much time to think about it," Austin admitted, sliding his arm across Jamie's shoulders. Jamie shifted to rest his head against Austin's chest.

"Brent Lawson said to tell you that everything he and Ben have compiled so far is all waiting for you on the secure drive, whenever you're ready to get started," Jamie said, feeling warm and sleepy. "Oh, and they came up with a fancy name for it—the Haven Project."

Austin chuckled. "Nice. I like it."

"The funding came through from that benefactor in Charleston," Jamie continued. "Everything's greenlighted. Looks like you've got a new job."

After Austin and Jamie uncovered the paranormal trafficking ring and underground rescue operation at Havenwood, they'd had a long conversation with Brent Lawson and another PI who knew about the supernatural, Ben Nolan. Along with Jamie's friend Simon Kincaide and others, they had decided to investigate disappearances over the same time period at sanitariums across the Northeast.

"On top of the *other* new job," Austin replied. Shortly after they arrived in Fox Hollow, Sheriff Armel stopped in to offer Austin a part-time role as a consultant. Turned out he knew both Ben and Simon, who urged Armel to recruit Austin because of his background as a cop, an investigator, and a psychic. Between the Haven Project and his new gig with the Fox Hollow's sheriff's department, Jamie knew Austin's mind rested easier about making a go of his relocation.

Simon and Brent also relayed some of the details and information Austin and Jamie had uncovered in Saranac Lake and passed it on to "friends." Things happened quickly. Not one person approached either of them about the deaths of Ed and Winters. They never got details on what Isabel's clean-up had entailed and decided it was probably best not to ask since it had worked out to their benefit. Jamie's resignation went somewhat unnoticed once the scandal hit about his boss being charged with money laundering and fraud. Soon after, the crooked sheriff and several of his deputies were under investigation themselves.

Jamie still felt bad for Quincey. He'd died unexpectedly the same day Jamie had last seen him, and Jamie knew he would always wonder if the ghosts from the Historical Association played a role, angry about Quincey's part in the kidnapping.

"I'm not sure how I went from doing a favor for my grandma to being recruited into a group of supernatural sleuths, but I'm not complaining," Austin joked.

Jamie could see Austin's excitement about the projects and his curiosity about the hunters and hackers he was likely to meet. The need to stay under the radar to avoid being noticed by some shadowy secret Vatican and government groups just added to the challenge.

"Just think, I can quit chasing cheating husbands and insurance fraud and do something that actually matters," Austin said.

"Even better, you'll be here, with me, for good." Jamie slid his hand up Austin's leg to where his fiancé was plumping quickly in his jeans.

"Mm," Austin said, pulling Jamie to straddle his lap and running his hands up and down Jamie's back. "I can think of some wild and wicked things we can do now that I'm home."

Jamie ground down against him and leaned in for another kiss. "I'm very good at being wild and wicked," he whispered, laying a trail of kisses down Austin's jaw to his throat. "Let's get comfortable in bed, and I'll give you a homecoming you'll never forget."

THE MAGIC EMPORIUM

For the One Thing You Didn't Know You Needed

Welcome to the Magic Emporium, a magic shop that can appear in any world or realm. It never shows up in the same place twice, and it only appears for creatures in dire need of one of its magical items. How is dire need defined? Depends on who's telling the story.

Haven was originally part of the Magic Emporium series. Though the series has now disbanded, these were the other titles linked in the series linked by the concept. They can all be read as standalone.

- **Knight and Day** by Jacki James
- **Brought to Light** by Eliot Grayson
- **A Dragon's Fortune** by Sam Burns & W.M. Fawkes
- **The Muffin Man** by Kim Fielding
- **Hexes and Horns** by Rowan McAllister
- **Must Love Demons** by Meghan Maslow
- **Elven Duty** by Rhys Lawless
- **The Young Man's Guide to Love and Loyalty** by Clara Merrick
- **Geoffrey the Very Strange** by Angel Martinez
- **Purgatory Playhouse** by EJ Russell
- **Stop Dragon My Heart Around** by Ari McKay & Rachel Langella
- **Haven** by Morgan Brice

AFTERWORD

I hope you enjoyed getting to meet Austin and Jamie. If you want to learn more about Fox Hollow, check out *Huntsman*, the first in my Fox Hollow: Zodiac series. While *Imaginary Lover* and *Haven* aren't direct sequels, they are set in the same fictional town and include a number of characters you'll meet again and again.

Psychic medium Simon Kincaide stars in his own series, Badlands, set in Myrtle Beach, where he teams up with a skeptical homicide cop to solve supernatural murders. Ben Nolan is one of the main characters in my Treasure Trail series, set in Cape May, NJ. Brent Lawson and his partner Travis Dominick have their own series as well, The Night Vigil, starting with Sons of Darkness (written under my Gail Z. Martin name). And the "benefactor from Charleston" is part of my Deadly Curiosities series (also written as Gail Z. Martin).

All of my modern-day series as Morgan Brice and Gail Z. Martin overlap, and the characters know each other, help each other, and show up in each other's books.

The Adirondacks are one of my favorite places, and I grew up going camping there for many years. It's a beautiful area, and I love getting to share it with all of you through the books.

Thank you for reading. Because you read, I write.

ABOUT THE AUTHOR

Morgan Brice is the romance pen name of bestselling author Gail Z. Martin. Morgan writes urban fantasy male/male paranormal romance, with plenty of action, adventure, and supernatural thrills to go with the happily ever after.

Gail writes epic fantasy and urban fantasy, and together with co-author hubby Larry N. Martin, steampunk and comedic horror, all of which have less romance and more explosions.

On the rare occasions Morgan isn't writing, she's either reading, cooking, or spoiling a very pampered dog.

Watch for additional new series from Morgan Brice and more books in the Witchbane, Badlands, Treasure Trail, Kings of the Mountain, Sharps & Springfield, and Fox Hollow universes coming soon!

Where to find me, and how to stay in touch

Join my Worlds of Morgan Brice Facebook Group and get in on all the behind-the-scenes fun! My free reader group is the first to see cover reveals, learn tidbits about works-in-progress, have fun with exclusive contests and giveaways, find out about in-person get-togethers, and more! It's also where I find my beta readers, ARC readers, and launch team! Come join the party! https://www.Facebook.com/groups/WorldsOfMorganBrice

Find me on the web at https://morganbrice.com. Sign up

for my newsletter and never miss a new release! http://
eepurl.com/dy_8oL. You can also find me on Twitter: @Mor-
ganBriceBook, on Pinterest (for Morgan and Gail): pinter-
est.com/Gzmartin, on Instagram as MorganBriceAuthor, on
YouTube at https://www.youtube.com/c/GailZMartinAu
thor/ on Bookbub https://www.bookbub.com/authors/
morgan-brice and now on TikTok @MorganBriceAuthor

Check out the ongoing, online convention ConTinual
www.facebook.com/groups/ConTinual

Support Indie Authors

When you support independent authors, you help influence what kind of books you'll see and what types of stories
will be available because the authors themselves decide
what to write, not a big publishing conglomerate. Independent authors are local creators supporting their families
with the books they produce. Thank you for supporting
independent authors and small press fiction!

ALSO BY MORGAN BRICE

Badlands Series

Badlands

Restless Nights, a Badlands Short Story

Lucky Town, a Badlands Novella

The Rising

Cover Me, a Badlands Short Story

Loose Ends

Night, a Badlands Short Story

Leap of Faith, A Badlands/Witchbane Novella

No Surrender

Point Blank

Fox Hollow Zodiac Series

Huntsman

Again

Fox Hollow Universe

Romp

Nutty for You

Imaginary Lover

Haven

Gruff

Kings of the Mountain series

Kings of the Mountain

The Christmas Spirit, a Kings of the Mountain Short Story

Sins of the Fathers

Sharps & Springfield Series

Peacemaker

Treasure Trail Series

Treasure Trail

Blink

Treasure Trail Universe

Light My Way Home, a Treasure Trail Novella

Witchbane Series

Witchbane

Burn, a Witchbane Novella

Dark Rivers

Flame and Ash

Unholy

The Devil You Know

The Christmas Crunch, a Witchbane Short Story

Sandwiched, Witchbane Short Story